Lucretia Maria Davidson

Poems by Lucretia Maria Davidson

Lucretia Maria Davidson

Poems by Lucretia Maria Davidson

ISBN/EAN: 9783743308664

Manufactured in Europe, USA, Canada, Australia, Japa

Cover: Foto ©Andreas Hilbeck / pixelio.de

Manufactured and distributed by brebook publishing software
(www.brebook.com)

Lucretia Maria Davidson

Poems by Lucretia Maria Davidson

your aff. brother

L. P. Davidson

Your affectionate Sister
L. M. Dawson

POEMS

BY

LUCRETIA MARIA DAVIDSON.

WITH ILLUSTRATIONS BY F. O. C. DARLEY.

EDITED BY M. OLIVER DAVIDSON.

NEW YORK:
PUBLISHED BY HURD AND HOUGHTON.
Cambridge: Riverside Press.
1871.

RIVERSIDE, CAMBRIDGE:

STEREOTYPED AND PRINTED BY

H. O. HOUGHTON AND COMPANY.

CONTENTS.

———

CONTENTS.

(. 112
113
16

LIST OF ILLUSTRATIONS.

———◆———

INTRODUCTORY.

" A thing of beauty is a joy forever :
 Its loveliness increases ; it will never
 Pass into nothingness."

In bringing out at this time a new edition of the poems of one of the sweetest and most intellectual spirits that this country ever knew ; in introducing to an entirely new generation of readers the writings of one who for forty-five years has lain beneath the lilies and the violets in a quiet country church-yard on the borders of Lake Champlain, we feel that we are performing a worthy act which cannot but be fully appreciated and acknowledged.

The simple fact that a young girl of less than seventeen summers, should have written the poems contained in this volume, was, and would be even at this time, something remarkable, especially when we remember that in those days there were but few female poets in the land, and none who could have laid claim, at so early an age, to such tender and thoughtful effusions. It is sad to think that this young girl, so talented and so filled with inspiration ; who seemed to be imbued with the very spirit and essence of poesy, and who gave such excellent promise and token of a glorious career, should have so early passed away. Had she lived until womanhood, who can tell what she might have accomplished! Without being a great poet, she yet possessed all the attributes of one, and many of her earliest productions contained evidences of poetic power, which needed only culture and proper guidance — which, had her health and years permitted, she would have received — to have made her the peeress of the fairest poets of the land. As it is, we can only speak of her as a child — a wondrous child, though ; sensitive to excess, and thoughtful beyond her years. Precocious, too, though not through study, but by nature ; she seemed intuitively to know things which puzzle ofttimes the learned ; though where or how she gained her knowledge, was a mystery even to those by whom she was daily surrounded, — her parents, her teachers, and her friends.

Her productions were not, as one might think, the result entirely of laborious work ; many of them were born on the inspiration of the moment, when the divine afflatus was full upon her ; and yet others were the result of careful thought and study ; but however this was, their composition was always to her a heartfelt pleasure. Other children of her years would find their chief enjoyment in play ; but she was never happier than when engaged in composing a poem which was as much a recreation to her as it would have been a task to most others.

As a poet, Lucretia Davidson possessed a depth of

thought, a delicacy of expression, a tenderness of senti-
ment, and an appreciation of melody rarely to be met.
She had a fine fancy, a quick imagination, a quiet and
unobtrusive humor, and underlying all a foundation of
thorough and unwavering thoughtfulness. Her writings
are marked by grace, ease, and refinement, and evince
not only a catholic but a classical taste. Her heart as
well as her mind, is apparent in her compositions ; and
soul, as well as intellect, permeates and gives character to
her productions.

But the genius of Lucretia Davidson has been acknowledged by writers greatly distinguished in literature,
not only in this country but in England. Robert
Southey, one of the most brilliant critics and accomplished poets, wrote in praise of her productions years
ago, in the " London Quarterly Review." With a full-
ness of expression, creditable to his heart as well as to
his understanding, he said : " In these poems there is
enough of originality, enough of aspiration, enough of
conscious energy, enough of growing power, to warrant
any expectations, however sanguine, which the patrons
and the friends and parents of the deceased could have
formed."

It is not our intention to write a biography of Lucretia
Davidson. This has, as will be seen by referring to the
appendix at the close of this volume, already been done
so fully and successfully, by a distinguished pen, — that
of Miss Sedgwick, — as to leave little for any one else to
do. We purpose, therefore, to add only a few simple

facts, obtained from her only surviving brother, M. O. Davidson, Esq., of Westchester County, in relation to other members of the Davidson family — her mother and a brother, both now deceased — who possessed in no small degree the divine art of clothing their thoughts in the garb of poesy.

Of Mrs. Davidson we need only say that she was a woman of elegant culture and refinement, gifted with a superior mind, and possessing great beauty of face and figure. For many years previous to her death, which occurred in 1844, she had been in delicate health, and was at times a confirmed invalid. Between the mother and her two gifted daughters the most perfect sympathy of tastes, feelings, and pursuits existed. Their hearts and minds were indissolubly twined together, and a more beautiful relationship of both a maternal and filial character never existed.

It was to Mrs. Davidson that Mrs. Caroline Southey, the wife of the laureate, addressed the following touching lines, written at Greta Hall, Keswick, Cumberland, England, and bearing date April 10th, 1842 : —

TO THE MOTHER OF LUCRETIA AND MARGARET DAVIDSON.

O lady, greatly favored, greatly tried !
  Was ever glory, ever grief like thine,
  Since hers, the mother of the Man divine,
The perfect One — the Crowned — the Crucified ?
Wonder and joy, high hopes and chastened pride

Thrilled thee ; intently watching, hour by hour,
　The fast unfolding of each human flower,
In hues of more than earthly brilliance dyed.
And then — the blight, the fading, the first fear,
　The sickening hope, the doom, the end of all :
Heart withering, if indeed all ended here.
　But from the dust, the coffin, and the pall,
Mother bereaved, thy tearful eyes upraise,
Mother of angels, join their songs of praise !

As we have before said, a son of this gifted and accomplished woman was also a poet and one of no slight
ability.　For several years previous to his death, he con-
tributed to the pages of the "Southern Literary Messenger" and other periodicals of the day.　To him we
are indebted for the completion of a poem, "The Parting of Decourcy and Wilhelmine," left unfinished by
Lucretia at the time of her death, and found by her
mother among her manuscripts.　That portion of it —
from the seventeenth to the last stanza inclusive — mentioned in the original edition of the poems as being
furnished by another hand, is from the pen of Lieutenant
Davidson.　It is marked by greater vigor, and displays
a fuller acquaintance with the subject — carrying out,
however, the same idea initiated by Lucretia — than she,
with all her innate knowledge and appreciation of the
same, could have hoped to have given to it.　Indeed, it
breathes in every line a soldierly spirit.

A brief sketch of this brother of Lucretia, with a
selection from his writings, will not, we trust, be unin-
teresting to the readers of this volume.

Lieut. L. P. Davidson, U. S. A., was born in 1816, at Plattsburg, N. Y. He was educated for Middlebury College under the care of the Rev. Canon Townsend, Rector of the parish of St. George and St. Thomas, a scholar of rare abilities, who is still living at Clarenceville, Canada East. Young Davidson, at an early age, became partial to classical lore. He translated and versified several of the books of Virgil, and filled a number of manuscript volumes with original poems and translations from both Latin and Greek poets.

In the year 1831 he entered Middlebury College, where he remained two years, until 1833, when he was transferred to the United States Military Academy at West Point, appointed at large by General Jackson, through the representations of the late General Macomb, to whom his talents had greatly recommended him. He graduated in 1837, in the same class with Sedgwick, Hooker, Vogdes, Benham, and other officers subsequently greatly distinguished in the Mexican war and the war of the great Rebellion. On the formation of the 1st regiment of dragoons, at his own request, he was assigned to this branch of the service, and immediately entered upon active duty on the western frontier.

While in the service he did much to elevate the moral as well as the military standing of the soldier, and, among other good works, advocated the establishment of "post libraries," and wrote several songs of a stirring character, in praise of a soldier's life, especially such a life as could only be found in the excitement and dangers

incident to the far West. These songs were, and some
of them doubtless still are, sung about the camp-fires
of the cavalry; while others were for the recruiting
service, and ofttimes effectively served the intended purpose, inducing many a brave fellow to enlist under the
flag of his country. A favorite one was called "The
Light Dragoon." It was dedicated to Lieut. A. R.
Johnston, and published, if we mistake not, by the old
firm of Firth and Hall, of New York, in 1841. Although
the dragoon branch of the service has been abolished
and the cavalry substituted in its stead, this song, with
its dashing chorus, has not been allowed to pass away.
It read as follows : —

THE LIGHT DRAGOON.

I.

Good cheer, my steed,
Let thy headlong speed,
Dash the dew from the prairie grass,
Shrink not, my horse,
Let the hills fall back,
As the ranks of our squadrons pass.
Then up, gallant steed, the wild wind's speed
Is but slow to thy headlong flight,
And we'll rein up soon, and the light dragoon,
With his charger will sleep to-night.

II.

At the fall of night,
In the gray twilight,
When I've combed thy tangled mane,

'Neath the smile of the moon,
Then the light dragoon
Will lie down by his steed again.
Then up, gallant steed, etc.

III.

When sleep is done,
And the rising sun
Shall have burnished thy glossy hair,
To horse again,
And we'll scour the plain,
And we'll beat up the red man's lair.
Then up, gallant steed, etc.

It is to be regretted that Lieut. Davidson should have
destroyed, shortly before his death, nearly his entire
collection of manuscript poems ; for, if we may trust the
judgment of those of his friends who had read them,
many possessed more than a common degree of merit.
From a few which escaped the flames, we select one, not
so much for the poetic skill displayed in its composition,
as for the interest of the story connected with it, and
which serves to introduce an incident in the life of its
writer.

Lieut. Davidson possessed a favorite charger named
" Chicago," which had carried him on many a weary
march, and through many a dangerous defile in the Indian country. For its docility and almost human intel-
ligence, it was fondly loved by the soldier, who regarded
it with a like affection that the Arab of the desert is
said to have for his steed.

In one of the wild skirmishes with the Indians, "Chicago" was killed by an arrow, and in falling confined his rider to the ground. The savages swept down to secure the tempting scalp, but were arrested by the fall of their leader, shot by a sergeant, also dismounted, who ran to the assistance of his officer, and delivered his fire over the dead body of the horse.

The Lieutenant, mourning the loss of his valued steed and companion, after the fight, to prevent him from becoming food for the wild animals of the prairie, buried him where he fell. These lines, written in pencil on the back of a blank requisition for holsters, bridle-bits, etc., were found, after Lieut. Davidson's death, in a pocket of his waistcoat : —

EPITAPH ON MY HORSE.

And thou art dead, my noble steed !
    The duties of a friend are done :
Thou wert the soldier's friend, indeed,
    And nobly has thy course been run.
That flashing eye, that lofty head,
Are dim, and spiritless, and dead,
    And stiffened are thy limbs of speed.

O ! if the bugle's stirring blast,
    With war's enlivening influence rife,
Could usher back the moments past,
    And raise the slumbering dead to life :
How quickly would'st thou prance again,
And limbs, and nerves, and sinews strain,
    To taste the raptures of the strife.

But round thy grave the western storm,
   With music harsh, and sad, and drear,
Will whistle o'er thy mouldering form,
   And howl its anthem o'er thy bier.
The panther's fangs shall harm thee not —
The prairie wolf shall pass the spot ;
   Too noble game for them lies here !

Quite different in its character, and evidently more carefully written, are the lines entitled " Longings for the West," composed a few months before his death ; but not published in the " Southern Literary Messenger " (from the pages of which we take them) until after his decease, namely, in the number for February, 1843, where they are prefaced by complimentary remarks from the editor.

LONGINGS FOR THE WEST.

O ! that the poet's mystic power were mine,
 Harmonious words in thrilling verse to join ;
What sweeter music than to strike the chords,
To paint the beauties of the West in words,
And sing in praise that sweetest spot of earth,
Home of the wild and free, — dear Leavenworth.
Be still, my heart ! let mem'ry's touch divine,
Bring back past joys to glad this soul of mine,
And spread the kindly veil o'er doubt and pain.
I would not call back grief's but pleasure's form again.
How oft I've sat in melancholy mood,
Where mad Missouri rolls his reckless flood,
To watch the mighty stream with wond'ring eye,

Born of a mountain spring to swell the sea,
And to man's life compare the aspiring wave, —
" Is born, is great," then thunders to the grave.
I turn my eyes, the sun's departing beam
Gilds yonder hill with more than earthly gleam ;
It glows like Sinai's mount, then fades to gloom.
Ambitious, soaring child, it typifies thy doom.
Oft when the morn smiled bright o'er frosty ground,
And startling horn had waked the slumbering hound,
I've sprung to horse, and with the shouting train,
Chased fox and wolf o'er hill and dale and plain,
Till tired with sport I've checked my headlong steed,
Where some bright stream winds through the flow'ry mead,
And thrown me down, where sunbeams never come.
To rest, to sleep, perchance to dream of home,
Or watch my horse with eager ear and eye,
Start at the hounds' deep bay, and hunters' distant cry :
Days, weeks and months, I've coursed the prairie's plain,
Garden of God ! the red man's rich domain —
Oft chilled by cold, or scorched by summer's sun,
From morn till night, till many a march was done,
Then laid me down in some wild Indian's camp,
The earth my resting-place, cold, drear, and damp,
To watch the stars — to mark the sullen owl,
To catch the cadence of the wolf's sad howl,
Or list the tales of scout and foray far,
Of skulking Pawnee band, or murderous Delaware, —
O ! could I catch that martial strain again,
The band's wild music thrilling through each vein,
While deep-mouthed trumpets rich alarums pour ;
'Twere worth a life to hear those sounds once more.

O ! could I see one moment, scan again
The bright parade, the soldiers' glittering train,
Watch every movement, mark with rapture's eye,
Each marshalled squadron as its ranks pass by,
And if at speed the mimic field they scour,
To join the rushing ranks, and shout the charge once more !

Spirit of memory, gentler pictures bring,
And teach my Muse of social joys to sing :
Of winter evenings, long from close of day,
With comrades passed in converse grave and gay,
While tales of daring, wear the lengthened night,
Of border warfare, or of Indian fight :
Teach me to sing the glad and social dance,
Where waltzers whirl and bright eyes witching glance,
While friends in cities mourn our hapless lot,
As banished exiles here, sad, desolate, forgot.

After five years' active service on the plains, during
which time he was exposed to many dangers and hardships, his health began to fail him, and he was obliged
to ask a furlough. His native air, however, and the
quietude of home-life failed to restore to him his fading
health : and hoping to find abroad what he could not in
this country, he visited Europe, explored Greece, where
were laid the scenes of his favorite poets, and also travelled
in Malta and Syria, returning through Italy and France.
But all to no purpose ; and, with feebler steps and a more
wasted frame than when he bade farewell to home and
friends, he came back only to die. His death took place

in June, 1842, and his remains were interred in the burial-ground at Saratoga.

The following lines, slightly varied from a stanza of the original poem — " The Mother's Lament" — written by Lucretia, are inscribed on his tombstone : —

> " Calmly he rests on a bosom far colder
>   Than that which once pillowed his health-blushing cheek ;
> Calmly he rests there, to silently moulder,
>   No tear to disturb him, no sigh to awake."

Lieutenant Davidson was possessed of a high, chivalric nature. He was brave, magnanimous, and full of charity. He was of that type and mould of character of which soldiers are made, and General Scott never spoke more truthfully than when, on hearing of his death, he said : " The army has lost one of its brightest ornaments." Had he lived, he would doubtless have attained high rank in the army, and been honored as a patriot, a soldier, and a man.

His portrait, engraved on steel, graces this volume.

In addition to what we have already said in relation to Lucretia Davidson, we desire to quote a few remarks written by Mrs. Davidson, in her dedication to Washington Irving of a former edition of these poems, published in 1841, detailing the circumstances under which several of the poems were written.

" I have felt," Mrs. Davidson wrote, " much diffidence in presenting these manuscripts to the public, in their present imperfect and unfinished state ; but the circum-

stances under which many of them were written, condemned, and partly destroyed by herself, as if unworthy
to hold a place among her papers, her extreme youth and
loveliness, and the melancholy fact of her dying before
she had time to complete others, will, I trust, make them
not less interesting to the reader of taste and feeling.

" The allegory of ' Alphonso in search of Learning,'
was written at the age of eleven. It was suggested to
her infant mind by seeing a cupola erected upon the
Plattsburg Academy, upon which was painted the Temple of Science.

" The poem of ' Chicomico ' was written after a severe
illness which confined me many months to my bed,
during which time Lucretia made a resolution that if I
ever should recover, she would give up her ' scribbling,'
as she called it, and devote herself to me ; at my earnest
entreaty, however, she resumed her pen, and the first
thing she produced was ' Chicomico,' prefaced by the following lines : —

" ' I had thought to have left *thee*, my sweet harp, forever ;
   To have touched thy dear strings again — never — O, never.
   To have sprinkled oblivion's dark waters upon thee,
   To have hung thee where wild winds would hover around thee ;
   But the voice of affection hath called forth one strain,
   Which, when sung, I will leave thee to silence again.'

" This beautiful tribute of affection has ever been one
of the most cherished relics of my child, and I deeply
regret that the irregular and unconnected state of the
manuscript obliges me to withhold the whole of the first
part.

" The ballad of ' Decourcy and Wilhelmine ' was written for a weekly paper, which she issued for the amusement of the family. It was dated from 'The Little Corner of the World,' edited by the Story-Teller, and dedicated to Mamma. After a time it was discontinued, and to my extreme regret destroyed. The fragment inserted in the collection, is one of the very few remnants found among her manuscripts ; the first sixteen verses are purely original ; the sequel was supplied by a friend, it being deemed too fine to be rejected for want of mere filling out. Lucretia's diffidence, and the apprehension that the circumstances might transpire or the papers be read by some friend out of the family, was, I believe, the sole reason why she discontinued and destroyed them. This mutilated paper, and a part of ' Rodin Hall,' are all that remain of the ' Story-Teller.'

" Her sweetly playful disposition is strongly manifested in her ' Petition of the Old Comb.' She had retired to her room with her books and pen, where she had spent several days. Feeling a desire to see how she was getting on, I went to her room. As I passed through the hall, I saw a sealed letter directed to me, lying at the foot of the stairs ; I opened it, and found it contained the

"PETITION OF A POOR OLD COMB."

" ' Dear mistress, I am old and poor,
    My teeth decayed and gone ;
O, give me but one moment's rest,
    For, mark, I'm tott'ring down.

" ' Thy raven locks, for many a day,
    I've bound around thy brow ;
And now that I am old and lame,
    I prithee let me go.

" ' Have I not, many a weary hour,
    Peep'd o'er thy book or pen,
And seen what this poor mangled form
    Will ne'er behold again ?

" ' A faithful servant I have been,
    But ah ! my day is past ;
And all my hope, and all my wish,
    Is liberty at last.

" ' Mark but the glittering, well-filled shelf
    Where my companions lie ;
Are they not fairer than myself,
    And younger far than I ?

" ' O ! then in pity hie thee there,
    Where thousands wait thy call,
And twine one in thy raven hair,
    To shroud my shameful fall.

" ' My days are hast'ning to their close,
    Crack ! crack ! goes every tooth ;
A thousand pains, a thousand woes,
    Remind me of my youth.

" ' Adieu then — in distress I die —
    My last hold fails me now ;

Adieu, and may thy elf locks fly
Forever 'round thy brow.'

"On reading it, I went up-stairs, and found her enveloped in books and manuscripts. Several large folios
lay open on the table, to which she seemed to have been
referring; while books, papers, and scraps of poetry were
strewn in confusion over the carpet. Her luxuriant
hair had escaped from its confinement, and hung in rich
glossy curls upon her neck and shoulders, while the
superannuated comb lay at her feet. As I hastily entered the room, she manifested some mortification, that I
should have surprised her in the midst of so much confusion, and, throwing her handkerchief over her papers,
laughingly asked what I thought of the Petition? I advised her to send directly to the ' well-filled glittering
shelf,' as I had no desire to see the curse denounced
verified, or her

"Elf locks fly
Forever 'round her brow."

"'Maritorne, or the Pirate of Mexico,' was written in
Albany, during her stay at the Institution of Miss
Gilbert, at a time when she was ill, in the brief space of
three weeks, while getting daily lessons like any other
school-girl. During that period, she also produced several fugitive pieces. She had been absent from home
but six weeks when I was summoned to attend her: she
had then been confined to her bed three weeks. On the
morning after my arrival, she desired me to collect the

scattered sheets of 'Maritorne,' and expressed much sorrow when she found that some were missing. She told me, with tears, that she feared she could never supply the loss, and said, ' Do, mamma, take care of what remains : it is thus far the best thing I ever wrote.'

" After her death, in her portfolio, which her nurse told me she used every day, sitting in bed, supported by pillows, I found the ' Last Farewell to my Harp,' and the ' Fear of Madness,' both written in a feeble, irregular hand, and evidently under a state of strong mental excitement. By their side lay the unfinished head of a Madonna, copied from a painting executed several centuries ago, and with the drawing lay also the unfinished poem suggested by the painting : —

> ' Roll back, thou tide of time, and tell.'

" In the ' Last Farewell to my Harp,' the presentiment of her death, if I may so term it, is strongly portrayed, mingled with the feeling of presumption which she often manifested in having 'dared to gaze

> ' Upon the lamp which never can expire,
> The undying, wild, poetic fire.'

" There is something extremely touching in the last stanzas : —

> ' And here, my harp, we part forever ;
> I'll waken thee again — O ! never ;
> Silence shall chain thee cold and drear,
> And thou shalt calmly slumber here ! '

" ' The Fear of Madness.' — The reader will find his sympathies all awakened upon perusing this unfinished fragment from the pen of the lovely sufferer. It leaves too painful a sensation upon the mind to admit a comment."

It only remains for us to add to this slight sketch, that the author of this volume of poems died in 1825, just a month before her seventeenth birthday. The following inscription appears on a modest marble monument erected over her remains in the family burial-ground at Plattsburg : —

LUCRETIA M. DAVIDSON
WAS BORN SEPT. 27, 1808,
AND
DIED AUGUST 27, 1825,
AGED 16 YEARS AND 11 MONTHS

" Here innocence and beauty lies, whose breath
Was snatched by early, not untimely death." — POPE.

On another side of the stone appear these beautiful lines from the pen of Mr. Bryant : —

" In the cold, moist earth we laid her,
When the forests cast the leaf,
And we wept that one so lovely
Should have a life so brief ;

" Yet not unmeet it was that one,
Like that young friend of ours,
So gentle and so beautiful,
Should perish with the flowers."

The opposite side of the marble bears these words : —
" This monument was raised as a testimony of affection by her mourning father."

This volume, so handsomely gotten up, and in the illustration of which the pencil of a distinguished artist has been employed, is a tribute of affection from an only surviving brother to the memory of a beloved sister.

In arranging this book for publication, we have brought together, as far as practicable, the miscellaneous poems in the order of the years in which they were written ; the first one being dated in 1819, when the author was in her eleventh year. It should be understood that the date of each year is prefixed to only one of the poems ; and all those that follow it, until the next date appears, were written during the said named year.

In the biographical sketch by Miss Sedgwick, we have omitted a few paragraphs, not deemed relevant, at this time, to the complete understanding of Lucretia's life. We have also incorporated into the body of the work several poems which have heretofore appeared only in the pages of the biography.

It is proper here to state that a new edition of the poems of Margaret Davidson, the younger sister, uniform with this volume, is in preparation. The works of both of these sisters have long been out of print, and we have little doubt that these editions will be welcomed by many readers : the old, who knew and prized the poets long ago, and the new, to whom their poems will be a fresh and beautiful revelation. To them, therefore, we joyfully submit this volume. BARRY GRAY.

FORDHAM, N. Y., *July* 25, 1870.

AMIR KHAN.

PART I.

Brightly o'er spire, and dome, and tower,
The pale moon shone at midnight hour,
While all beneath her smile of light
Was resting there in calm delight:
Evening, with robe of stars, appears,
Bright as repentant Peri's tears,
And o'er her turban's fleecy fold
Night's crescent streamed with rays of gold;
While every crystal cloud of heaven
Bowed as it passed the queen of even.

Beneath, calm Cashmere's lovely vale [1]
Breathed perfumes to the sighing gale;
The amaranth and tuberose,
Convolvulus in deep repose,
Bent to each breeze which swept their bed,
Or scarcely kissed the dew, and fled;
The bulbul, with his lay of love, [2]
Sang, 'mid the stillness of the grove;
The gulnare blushed a deeper hue, [3]
And trembling shed a shower of dew,

1

Which perfumed, ere it kissed the ground,
Each zephyr's pinion hovering round;
The lofty plane-tree's haughty brow [1]
Glittered beneath the moon's pale glow;
And wide the plantain's arms were spread, [5]
The guardian of its native bed.

Where was Amreta at this hour?
Say! was she slumbering in her bower?
Or gazing on this scene of rest,
Less calm, less peaceful than her breast?
Or was she resting in the dream
Of brighter days, on Fortune's stream?
Or was she weeping Friendship broken,
Or sighing o'er Love's withered token?

No! she was calmly resting there:
Her eye ne'er spoke of hope nor fear,
But 'mid the blaze of splendor round,
Forever bent upon the ground,
Their long dark lashes hid from view
The brilliant glances which they threw;
Her cheek was neither pale nor red;
The rose, upon its summer bed,
Could never boast so faint a hue —
So faint, and yet so brilliant too!

Though round her Cashmere's incense streamed;
Though Persia's gems around her beamed;
Though diamonds of Golconda shed
Their warmest lustre o'er her head;

Though music lulled each fear to sleep,
Or, like the night-wind o'er the deep,
Just waking love and calm delight,
Kindling Hope's watch-fire clear and bright —
For her, though Cashmere's roses twine
Together round the parent vine ;
And though to her, as Cashmere's star,
Knelt the once haughty Subahdar ;[6]
Still, still, Amreta gazed unmoved,
Nor sighed, nor smiled, nor owned she loved !
But, like the Parian marble there,
So bright, so exquisitely fair,
She seemed by Nature famed to bless,
Rich in surpassing loveliness.
But never from those lips of red
A single syllable had fled,
Since Amir Khan first blessed the hour [7]
That placed Amreta in his bower.
Within that bower, 'mid twining roses,
Upon whose leaves the breeze reposes,
She sits unmoved, while round her flow
Strains of sweet music, sad and low ;
Or now, in softer numbers breathing,
A song of love and sorrow wreathing,
Such strains as in wild sweetness ran
Through the sad breast of Amir Khan !

He loved, — and O ! he loved so well
That sorrow scarce dared break the spell ;
Though oft Suspicion whispered near
One vague, one sadly boding fear,

A fear that Heaven in wrath had made
That face with seraph-charms arrayed,
And then denied in mockery there
To breathe upon a face so fair!
Without that spark of heavenly flame,
Which burns unchanging, still the same;
Without that bright ethereal charm;
O! what were beauty's angel form?

The breeze as it sweeps o'er the poisonous flower,
Dripping with night's damp, blistering shower,
Laden with woe, disease, and death,
Fading youth's bloom with its passing breath,
Blighting each flower of various hue,
Ne'er o'er its fated victim threw
So dark a shade, a cloud so drear,
As hovered o'er the Subahdar.

Cool and refreshing sighs the breeze
Through the long walk of tzinnar-trees,[8]
And cool upon the water's breast
The pale moon rocks herself to rest, —
Yes! calmer, brighter, cooler far
Than the fevered brow of the Subahdar!

Amreta was fair as the morning beam,
As it glides o'er the wave of the Wuller's stream,[9]
But O! she was cold as the marble floor
That glitters beneath the nightly shower.

Where was that eye which none could scan,
Which once belonged to Amir Khan?

Where was that voice that mocked the storm?
Where was that tall, majestic form?
That eye was turned in love and woe
Upon Amreta's changeless brow;
That haughty form was bending low:
That voice was uttering vow on vow,
Beneath the lofty plane-tree's shade,
Before that cold Circassian maid!

"O speak, Amreta! but one word!
Let one soft sigh confess I'm heard!
Those eyes (than those of yon gazelle
More bright) a tale of love might tell!
Then speak, Amreta! raise thine eye,
Blush, smile, or answer with a sigh."

But 'twas in vain: no sigh, no word
Told that his humble suit was heard;
Veiled 'neath their silken lashes there,
Her dark eyes glanced no answered prayer;
Upon her cheek no blush was straying,
Around her lip no smile was playing;
And calm despair reigned darkly now
O'er Amir Khan's deep-clouded brow.

What pity that so fair a form
Should want a heart with feeling warm!
What pity that an eye so bright
Should beam o'er Reason's clouded night!
And like a star on Mahmoud's wave,[10]
Should glitter o'er a dreary grave:

A dark abyss — a sunless day,
An endless night without one ray.

'Twas at that day, that silent hour,
When the tall poppy sheds its shower,
When all on earth, and all on high
Seemed breathing slumber's sweetest sigh;
At that calm hour when Peris love
To gaze upon the heaven above,
Whose portals, bright with many a gem,
Are closed — forever closed on *them;*
'Twas at this silent, solemn hour,
That, gliding from his summer bower,
The Subahdar with noiseless step
Steals like the night-breeze o'er the deep.

Where glides the haughty Subahdar?
Onward he glides to where afar
Proud Hirney-Purvet rears his head [11]
High above Cashmere's blooming bed,
And twines his turban's fleecy fold
With many a brilliant ray of gold,
Or places on his brow of blue
The crescent with its silver hue.

There, 'neath a plantain's sacred shade,
Which deep, and dark, and widely spread,
Al Shinar's high prophetic form
Held secret counsel with the storm;
His hand had grasped, with fearless might,
The mantle of descending night.

Such matchless skill the prophet knew,
Such wond'rous feats his hand could do,
That Persia's realm astonished saw,
And Cashmere's valley gazed with awe!

Low bowed the lofty Amir Khan,
Before the high and mighty man,
And bending o'er the Naptha's stream,
Which onward rolled its fiery gleam,
The Subahdar in murmurs told
Of beauteous form, of bosom cold,
Of rayless eye, of changeless cheek,
Of tongue which could or would not speak.

At length the mourner's tale had ceased,
He crossed his hands upon his breast :
He spoke no word, he breathed no sigh,
But keenly fixed his piercing eye
Upon Al Shinar's gloomy brow,
In all the deep despair of woe.
The Prophet paused ; his eye he raised,
And stern and earnestly he gazed,
As if to pierce the sable veil
Which would conceal the mournful tale ;
When, starting with a sudden blow,
He oped a portal dark and low,
Which shrouded from each mortal eye
Al Shinar's cavern broad and high ;
'Twas bright, 'twas exquisitely bright,
For founts of rich and living light
There poured their burning treasures forth,
Which sought again their parent earth.

Rich vases, with sweet incense streaming,
Mirrors a flood of brilliance beaming,
Fountain, and bath, and curling stream,
At every turn before them beam ;
And marble pillars, pure and cold,
And glittering roof, inlaid with gold,
And gems and diamonds met his view
In wild and rich profusion too ;
And had Amreta's smiles been given,
This place had been the Moslem heaven !

The Prophet paused ; while Amir Khan
Gazed, awe-struck, on the wond'rous man,
Al Shinar plucked a pale blue flower,
Which bent beneath the fountain's shower,
Then slowly turned towards Amir Khan,
And placed the treasure in his hand.

" Mark me !" he cried ; " this pensive flower,
Gathered at midnight's magic hour,
Will charm each passion of the breast,
And calm each throbbing nerve to rest ;
'Twill leave thy bounding bosom warm,
Yet set death's seal upon thy form ;
'Twill leave thee stiff, and cold, and pale,
A slumberer 'neath an icy veil,
But still shall Reason's conscious reign
Unbroken, undisturbed, remain,
And thou shalt hear, and feel, and know
Each sigh, each touch, each throb of woe!

"Go thou! and if Amreta be
  Worthy of love, and worthy thee,
  When she beholds thee pale and cold,
  Wrapped in the damp sepulchral fold;
  When her eye wanders for that glow
  Once burning on thy marble brow;
  Then, if her bosom's icy frame
  Hath ever warmed 'neath passion's flame,
  'Twill heave tumultuous as it glows
  Like Baikal's everlasting throes;
  And if, to-morrow eve, you press
  This pale cold floweret to your breast,
  Ere morning smiles, its spell will prove
  If that cold heart be worth thy love!

PART II.

THERE's silence in the princely halls,
  And brightly blaze the lighted walls,
  While clouds of musk and incense rise
  From vases of a thousand dyes,
  And roll their perfumed treasures wide,
  In one luxuriant, fragrant tide;
  And glittering chandeliers of gold,
  Reflecting fire from every fold,
  Hung o'er the shrouded body there,
  Of Cashmere's once proud Subahdar!
  The crystal's and the diamond's rays
  Kindled a wide and brilliant blaze;
  The ruby's blush, the coral's hue,

By Peris dipped in Henni's dew,
The topaz' rich and golden ray,
The opal's flame, the agate gray,
The amethyst of violet hue,
The sapphire with its heavenly blue,
The snow-white jasper sparkling there
Near the carbuncle's deepening glare,
The warm carnelian's blushing glow
Reflected back the brilliant flow
Of light, which in refulgent streams,
O'er hall, o'er bower, and fountain beams.

O'er beds of roses, bright with dew,
Unfolding modestly to view,
Each trembling leaf, each blushing breast,
In Cashmere's wildest sweetness dressed :
Through vistas long, through myrtle bowers
Where Amir Khan once passed his hours
In gazing on Amreta's face,
So full of beauty, full of grace,
Through veils of silver bright and clear,
It poured its softened radiance far ;
Or beamed in pure and milky brightness,
O'er urns of alabaster whiteness ;
Through Persian screens of glittering gold,
O'er many an altar's sacred fold,
Where to Eternity will blaze
The naphtha's never-fading rays,
The Gheber's fire which dieth never,
But burns, and beams, and glows forever !

'Twas silent: not a voice was heard —
No sigh, no murmur, not one word
Was echoed through that brilliant hall;
The spell of silence hung o'er all;
For there had paused the wing of death,
The midnight spirit's withering breath.

At that still hour no sound arose
To break the charm of deep repose;
The lake was glittering, and the breeze
Sighed softly through the tzinnar trees,
And kissed the Wuller's wave of blue,
Or sipped the gull's light trembling dew;
But not a murmur, not a sigh
Was wafted by the night-breeze by,
Through that wide hall and princely bower,
At midnight's calm and solemn hour!

O! where was Love his night-watch keeping!
Or was the truant sweetly sleeping?
Where was he at that hour of rest,
By him created, claimed, and blessed?
Where were the tears of Love, and Sorrow,
The sigh which Sympathy can borrow?
Where were regret, and chill despair?
Where was Amreta? — where, O where?

Hark! 'tis the night-breeze softly playing,
Through veils of glittering silver straying —
No! 'tis a step — so quick, so light,
That the wild flower which weeps at night,

Would raise again its drooping head,
To greet the footstep which had fled.

'Tis not the breeze which floats around,
Lifting the light veil from the ground :
No! 'tis a form of heavenly mien
Hath dared to draw the curtain's screen.

Dimly, behind the fluttering veil,
Which trembles in the breathing gale,
A form appears of seraph mould
As 'neath a light cloud's fleecy fold ;
The veil is drawn with hasty hand,
Loosed is the rich embroidered band ;   .
'Tis solemn solitude around,
There's not a murmur, not a sound, —
Again a snowy hand is seen,
Again is raised the silken screen,
And lo! with light and noiseless tread,
Amreta glided from its shade !

Her veil was fluttering in the air,
Her brow, as Parian marble fair,
Was glittering bright with many a gem
Set in a brilliant diadem ;
Her long dark hair was floating far,
Braided with many a diamond star ;
Her eye was raised, and O! that eye
Seemed only formed to gaze on high !
For O, more piercing bright its beam
Than diamonds 'neath Golconda's stream :

That angel-eye was only given
To look upon its native heaven!
The glow upon her cheek was bright,
But it came, and it fled like a meteor's light ;
A brilliant tear was still lingering there,
And O, it was shed for the Subahdar!

O'er every tear the maiden shed,
The heart of Amir Khan had bled ;
Now, Amir Khan, she weeps for thee,
O! what must be thy ecstasy ?
For Amir Khan Amreta weeps,
Yet Amir Khan unheeding sleeps !
Like crystal dew-drops purely glowing,
O'er his pale brow her tears are flowing ;
She wipes them with her veil away,
Less sacred far — less sweet than they!

Where was that eye whose ardent gaze
Had warmed her bosom with its rays?
Where was that glance of love and woe ?
Where was that proud heart's throbbing glow?
All, all was cold and silent there,
And all was death, and dark despair!
She hid her face, now cold and pale,
Within her sweetly scented veil ;
Then seized her lute, and a strain so clear,
So soft, so mournful arose on the air,
That O! it was sweet as the music of heaven
O'er a lost one returning, a sinner forgiven !
Such notes as repentance in sorrow might sing,
Notes wafted to heaven by Israfil's wing : —

SONG.

Star of the morning! this bosom was cold,
  When forced from my native shade,
And I wrapped me around in my mantle's fold,
  A mournful Circassian maid!

I vowed that rapture should never move
  This changeless cheek, this rayless eye,
I vowed to feel neither bliss nor love, —
  In silence to meet thee, and *then* to die!

Each burning sigh thy bosom hath breathed,
  Has been melting that chain away;
The galling chain which around me I wreathed,
  On the morn of that fatal day!

'Tis done! and this night I have broken the vow
  Which bound me in silence forever!
And thy spirit hath fled from a world of woe,
  To return again, never! O never!

My soul is sad! and my heart is weary!
  For thy bosom is cold to me;
Without thy smile the world is dreary,
  And I will fly with thee!

Together we'll float down eternity's stream,
  Twin stars on the breast of the billow,

The splendors of Paradise round us shall beam,
  And thy bosom shall be my pillow!

Then open thine arms, bright star of the morning!
  My grave in thy bosom shall be,
The glories of Paradise round us are dawning,
  My heaven is only with *thee!*

Hushed were the words, and hushed the song,
Which sadly, sweetly flowed along,
But Amir Khan's warm heart beat high,
Though closed and rayless was his eye;
And every note which struck his ear,
Whispered a hovering angel near;
And each warm tear that wet his cheek,
Her long-concealed regard bespeak;
His bosom bounded to be free,
And fluttered, — wild with ecstasy!
O! would the magic charm had passed!
Would that the morn would break at last!
But no, — it will not, may not be!
He is not, nor can yet be free!

But hark! Amreta's murmurs rise,
Sweet as the bird of Paradise;
She bowed her head, and deeply sighed,
" Yes, Amir Khan, I am thy bride!
And here the crimson hand of death

Shall wed us with a rosy wreath!
My blood shall join us as it flows,
And bind us in a deep repose!"

Beneath her veil a light is beaming,
A dagger in her hand is gleaming,
And livid was the light it threw,
A pale, cold, death-like stream of blue,
Around her form of angel brightness,
And o'er her brow of marble whiteness!

Awake! O Amir Khan, awake!
Canst thou not rouse thee for *her* sake?
Beside thee can Amreta stand,
The fatal dagger in her hand,
And canst thou still regardless lie,
And let thy loved Amreta die?
Awake! O Amir Khan, awake!
And rouse thee for Amreta's sake!

—Like lightning from a midnight cloud,
The Subahdar, from 'neath his shroud,
Burst the cold, magic, death-like band,
And snatched the dagger from her hand!
The maiden sunk upon his breast,
And deep and lengthened was her rest!
There was no sigh, no murmur there,
And scarcely breathed the Subahdar,
While almost fearing to be blest,
He clasped Amreta to his breast!
Deep buried in his mantle's fold,

He felt not that her cheek was cold ;
His own heart throbbed with pleasure's thrill,
But whispered not that *hers* was still!
— Yes! the wild flow of blissful joy.
Which, bursting, threatened to destroy,
Gave to her soul a rest from feeling ;
A transient torpor gently stealing
O'er beating pulse, and throbbing breast,
Had calmed her every nerve to rest ;
— But see! the tide of life returns,
Once more her cheek with rapture burns,
Once more her dark eye's heavenly beam
Pours forth its full and piercing gleam,
Once more her heart is bounding high,
Too full to weep — too blest to sigh !

1824.

2

CHICOMICO.

This Poem is founded on the following actual occurrences: During the Seminole war, Duncan M. Rimmon (the Rathmond of the poem), a Georgia militiaman, was captured by the Indians. Hillis-adjo, their chief, condemned him to death. He was bound; but while the instruments of torture were preparing, the tender-hearted daughter of Hillis-adjo (the Chicomico of the tale) threw herself between the prisoner and his executioners, and interceded with her father for his release. She was successful. His life was spared. In the progress of the war, however, it was the fate of the generous Hillis-adjo (the prophet Francis) himself to be taken a prisoner of war, and it was thought necessary to put him to death. These incidents Miss Davidson wrought up, with other characters (probably fictitious), to compose the whole of this poem. The *first part* of the poem is so incomplete, that it was thought best to introduce the reader immedi- to the *second part*. The war had broken out. Chicomico had solicited the presence of Ompahaw, a venerable chief, to aid her father Hillis-adjo against the whites, with Rathmond at their head. The battle is described, the Indians are victorious, and Rathmond is taken prisoner. Here the second part commences.

PART II.

What sight of horror, fear and woe,
Now greets chief Hillis-ha-ad-joe?
What thought of blood now lights his eye?
What victim foe is doomed to die?
For his cheek is flushed, and his air is wild,
And he cares not to look on his only child.

His lip quivers with rage, his eye flashes fire,
And his bosom beats high with a tempest of ire.
Alas! 'tis Rathmond stands a prisoner now,
Awaiting death from Hillis-ha-ad-joe,
　From Hillis-ha-ad-joe, the stern, the dread,
To whose vindicate, cruel, savage mind,
Loss after loss fast following from behind,
　Had only added thirst insatiate for blood;
And now he swore by all his heart held dear,
That limb from limb his victims he would tear.

But ah! young Rathmond's case what tongue can tell!
Upon his hapless fate what heart can dwell?
To die when manhood dawns in rosy light,
　To be cut off in all the bloom of life,
To view the cup untasted snatched from sight,
　Is sure a thought with horror doubly rife.
Alas, poor youth! how sad, how faint thy heart!
　When memory paints the forms endeared by love,
From these so soon, so horribly to part;
　O! it would almost savage bosoms move!
But unextinguished hope still lit his breast,
And aimless still, drew scenes of future rest!
Caught at each distant light which dimly gleamed,
Though sinking, 'mid the abyss o'er which it beamed,
Like the poor mariner, who, tossed around,
Strains his dim eye to ocean's farthest bound,
Paints, in each snowy wave, assistance near,
And as it rolls away, gives up to fear:
Dreads to look round, for death's on every side,
The lowering clouds above the ocean wide:

He wails alone — "and scarce forbears to weep,"
That his wrecked bark still lingers on the deep!

E'en to the child of penury and woe,
   Who knows no friend that o'er his grave will weep,*
Whose tears in childhood's hour were taught to flow,
   Looks with dismay across death's horrid deep!
Then, when suspended o'er that awful brink,
   Snatched from each joy, which opening life may give,
Who would not from the prospect shuddering shrink,
   And murmur out *one* hope-fraught prayer to live!
But, see! the captive now is dragged along,
While round him mingle yell and wild-war song!
The ring is formed around the high raised pile,
Fagots o'er fagots reared with savage toil;
The impatient warriors watch with burning brands,
To toss the death-signs from their ruthless hands!
Nearer, and nearer still the wretch is drawn,
All hope of life, of rescue, now is gone!
A horrid death is placed before his eyes;
In fancy *now* he sees the flames arise,
He hears the deafening yell which drowns the cry
Of the poor victim's last, dire agony!
His heart was sick, he strove in vain to pray
   To that great God, before whose awful bar
His lightened soul was soon to wing its way
   From this sad world to other realms afar!

He raised his eyes to heaven's blue arch above,
That pure retreat of mercy and of love;
When, lo! two fellow-sufferers caught his eye.

      * Campbell.

The prophet Montonoc *is doomed to die!*
His haughty spirit now must be brought low;
Long had he been the chieftain's direst foe:
The Indian's face was wrapped in mystic gloom,
As on they led him to his horrid doom.
A hectic flush upon his dark cheek burned,
His eye nor to the right nor left hand turned:
His lip nor quivered, nor turned pale with fear,
Though the death-note already met his ear.
Tall and majestic was his noble mien,
   Erect, he seemed to brave the foeman's ire,
His step was bold, his features all serene,
   As he approached the steep funereal pyre!

Close at his side, a figure glided slow,
Clad in the dark habiliments of woe,
Whose form was shrouded in a mantle's fold,
All, save one treacherous ringlet, — bright as gold.

The death-song's louder note shrill peals on high,
A signal that the victim soon must die!
While yell and war-note join the chorus still,
Till the wild dirge rebounds from hill to hill!
Rathmond now turned to snatch a last sad gaze,
Ere closed life's curtain o'er his youthful days;
When he beheld the dark, the piercing eye
Of Montonoc, the prophet doomed to die,
Bent upon *him* with such a steady gaze,
That not more fixed was death's own horrid glaze!
Then lifting his long swarthy finger high,
To where the sun's bright beams just tinged the sky

And o'er the parting day its glories spread,
Which was to close when their sad souls had fled, —
"White man," he cried, in low mysterious tone,
Caught but by Rathmond's listening ear alone,
" Ere the bright eye of *yon red orb* shall sleep,
This haughty chief his fallen tribe shall weep!"
He said no more : for lo! the death-yells cease.
'Tis hushed! no sound is echoed through the place.
The opening ring disclosed a female there,
In a rich mantle shrouded, save her hair,
Which, long and dark, luxuriant round her hung,
With many a clear white pearl and dew-drop strung.

She threw back the mantle which shaded her face,
   She spoke not, but looked the pale spirit of woe!
The angel of mercy, the herald of grace,
   Knelt the sorrowful daughter of Hillis-ad-joe!
" My father! my father!" the maiden exclaims,
" O doom not the white man to die 'midst the flames!
'Tis thy daughter who kneels, 'tis Chicomico sues,
Can my father, the friend of my childhood, refuse?
This heart is the white man's, with him will I die,
With him to the Great Spirit's mansion I'll fly;
The flames which to heaven will waft *his* pure soul,
Round the form of *thy* daughter encircling shall roll;
My life is *his* life — *his* fate shall be *mine;*
For *his* image around *thy child's* heart will entwine!

Man's breast may be cruel, and savage, and stern,
From the sufferings of others it heedless may turn;
To the pleadings of want, to the wan face of woe,

To the sorrow-wrung drops which around it may flow,
But 'twill melt like the snow on the Apennine's breast,
As the sunbeam falls light on its fancy-crowned crest,
When the voice of a *child* to its cold ear is given,
Filled with sorrow's sad notes like the music of heaven.

" Loose the white man," the king in agony cried,
" My child, what *you* plead for, can ne'er be denied!
The prisoner is *yours!* to enslave or to free!
I yield him, Chicomico, wholly to *thee;*
But remember!" he cried, while pride conquered his
        woe,
" Remember, thy father is Hillis-ad-joe!"
He frowned, and his brow, like the curtains of night,
Looked darker, when tinged by a moonbeam of light:
Chicomico saw — she saw, and with dread,
The storm, which returning, might burst o'er her head:
And quickly to Rathmond she turned with a sigh,
While a love-brightened tear veiled her heavenly eye.

" Go, white man, go! without a fear;
Remember you to *one* are dear;
Go! and may peace your steps attend;
Chicomico will be your friend.
To-morrow eve with us may close
Joyful, and free from cares or woes;
To-morrow eve may also end,
And find me here without a friend!
Remember then the Indian maid,
Whose voice the burning brand hath stayed!
But should I be, as now I am,

And thou in prison and in woe,
Think that this heart is still the same,
And turn thee to Chicomico!
Then, go! yes, go! while yet you may,
Dread death awaits you if you stay!
May the Great Spirit guard and guide
Your footsteps through the forest wide!"
She said, and wrapped her mantle near
Her fragile form, with hasty hand,
Just bowed her head, and shed one tear,
Then sped him to his native land.

The wind is swift, and mountain hart,
From huntsman's bow the feathered dart;
But swifter far the prisoner's flight,
When freed from dungeon-chains and night!
So Rathmond felt, but wished to show
How much he owed Chicomico;
But she had fled; she did not hear!
She did not mark the grateful tear
Which quivered in the hero's eye;
Nor did she catch the half-breathed sigh;
And Heaven alone could hear the prayer,
Which Rathmond's full heart proffered there.

PART III.

While swift on his way young Rathmond sped,
Death's horrors awaited those he fled.
Already were the prisoners bound, —

One word, and every torch would fly ;
No step was heard, nor feeblest sound,
   Save the death raven's wing on high !
The sign was given, each blazing brand
Like lightning shot from every hand ;
The crackling, sparkling fagots blazed, —
Then Montonoc his dark eye raised ;
He whistled shrill — an answering call
Told that each foeman then should fall !
Sudden a band of warriors flew
From earth, as if from earth they grew.
The brake, the fern, and hazel-down,
Blazed brightly in the sinking sun ;
Confusion, blood, and carnage then
Spread their broad pinions o'er the glen ;
The blazing brands were quenched in blood,
And Montonoc unshackled stood !
He paused one moment — dark he frowned,
By dire revenge and slaughter crowned ;
Then bent his bow, let loose the dart,
And pierced the foeman Chieftain's heart.
Yes, Montonoc, thy arrow sped,
For Hillis-ha-ad-joe is dead !

And now within their hidden tent,
The conquered make their sad lament ;
Before them lay their slaughtered king,
While slowly round they form the ring ;
Dread e'en in death, the Chieftain's form
Seemed made to stride the whirlwind storm ;
Upon his brow a dreadful frown
Still lingered as the warrior's crown ;

And yet it seemed as mortal ire
Still sparkled in that eye of fire,
And, blazing, soon should light the face
O'er which death's shadow held its place,
And like the lightning 'neath a cloud,
Shoot flaming from its sable shroud.
But, hark! low notes of sorrow break
The solemn calm, and o'er the lake,
Float on the bosom of the gale;
Hark! 'tis the Chieftain's funeral wail!

Fallen, fallen, fallen low
Lies great Hillis-ha-ad-joe!
To the land of the dead,
By the white man sped!
In his hunting garb they shall welcome him there,
To the land of the bow and the antlered deer!

Fallen is Hillis-ha-ad-joe!
Chant his death-dirge sad and slow;
In the battle he fell, in the fight he died,
And many a brave warrior sunk by his side.
In his hunting garb they shall welcome him there,
To the land of the bow and the antlered deer.

The sun is sinking in the deep,
Our "mighty fallen one" we weep;
Fallen is Hillis-ha-ad-joe!
The axe has laid our broad oak low!
In his hunting garb they shall welcome him there,
To the land of the bow and the antlered deer.

The last sad note had sunk on the breeze,
Which mournfully sighed among the dark trees,
When a form thickly shrouded, swift glided along,
But joined not her voice to the funeral song.
When the notes ceased, she knelt, and in accents of
    woe,
Besought the Great Spirit for Hillis-ad-joe.
Her words were but few, and her manner was wild,
For she was the slaughtered Chief's poor orphan child!
She raised her dark eye to the sun sinking red,
She looked, and that glance told that reason had fled!

Why does thy eye roll wild, Chicomico?
Why dost thou shake like aspen's quivering bough?
Why o'er that fine brow streams thy raven hair?
Read! for the "wreck of reason's written there!"
'Tis true! the storm was high, the surges wild,
And reason fled the Chieftain's orphan child!
Thou poor heart-broken wretch on life's wild sea,
Say! who is left to love, to comfort thee?
All, all are gone, and thou art left alone,
Like the last rose, by autumn rudely blown.

But she has fled, the wild and wingéd wind
Is by her left, long loitering far behind!
But whither has she fled? to wild-wood glen,
Far from the cares, the joys, the haunts of men!
Her bed the rock, her drink the rippling stream,
And murdered friends her ever constant dream!
Her wild death-song is wafted on the gale,
Which echoes round the Chieftain's funeral wail!

Her little skiff she paddles o'er the lake,
And bids "the Daughter of the Voice," awake!
From hill to hill the shrieking echoes run,
To greet the rising and the setting sun.

PART IV.

THE lake is calm, the sun is low,
The whippoorwill is chanting slow,
And scarce a leaf through the forest is seen
To wave in the breeze its rich mantle of green.
Fit emblem of a guiltless mind,
    The glassy waters calmly lie;
Unruffled by a breath of wind,
    Which o'er its shining breast may sigh!
The shadow of the forest there
    Upon its bosom soft may rest;
The eagle-heights, which tower in air,
    May cast their dark shades o'er its breast.

But hark! approaching paddles break
The stillness of that azure lake!
Swift o'er its surface glides the bark,
Like lightning's flash, like meteor spark
It seemed, as on the light skiff flew,
As it scarce kissed the wave's deep blue,
Which, dimpling round the vessel's side,
Sparkled and whirled in eddies wide!

Who guides it through the yielding lake?

Who dares its magic calm to break?
'Tis Montonoe! his piercing eye
  Is raised to where the western hill
Rears its broad forehead to the sky,
  Battling the whirlwind's fury still.

'Twas Montonoe, and with him there
Was that strange form, with golden hair!
Wrapped in the self-same garb, as when,
Surrounded by those savage men,
The stranger had, with Montonoe,
Been led before the blazing stake!
Swift, swift the light skiff forward flew,
Till it had crossed the waters blue;
Both leaped like lightning to the land,
And left the skiff upon the strand;
Far 'mid the forest then they fled,
And mingled with its dark brown shade.

The oak's broad arms in the breeze were creaking,
The bird of the gloomy brow was shrieking,
When a note on the night-wind was wafted along,
A note of the dead Chieftain's funeral song.
A form was seen wandering in frantic woe,
'Twas the maniac daughter of Hillis-ad-joe!
Her dark hair was borne on the night-wind afar,
And she sung the wild dirge of the Blood-hound of
      War!
She ceased when she came near the breeze-ruffled
      lake;
She ceased — was't the wind sighing o'er the long
      brake?

Was't the soft rippling wave? was't the murmur of
    trees,
Which, bending, were brushed by the wing of the
    breeze?
Ah, no! for she shrieked, as her piercing eye caught
A form which her frenzied brain never forgot!
'Twas Rathmond! yes, Rathmond before her now
    stood,
And he glanced his full eye on the child of the wood.

"Chicomico!" he cried, his voice sad and low,
"Chicomico! we are the children of woe!
O, come, then! O, come! and thy Rathmond's strong
    arm
Shall shelter thee ever from danger and harm;
'Tis true, I have loved with the passion of youth!
I have loved; and let Heaven attest with what truth!
But, Cordelia, thy ashes are mixed with the dead"—
(Here his eye flashed more fierce, and his pale cheek
    turned red)
"'Twas *thy* father, Chicomico — yes, 'twas *thy* sire,
Who kindled the loved saint's funereal pyre!
But, 'tis passed"—(and he crossed his cold, quivering
    hand
O'er a brow that was burning like Zahara's sand,)
"'Tis passed! and Chicomico, *thou* didst preserve
The life of a wretch, who now never can love!
That life is thy own, with a heart, that though chilled
To passion's soft throb, is with gratitude filled!"

.   .   .   .

She turned her dark eye, from which reason's bright
    fire

Had fled, with the ghosts of her friends—of her sire;
"Young Eagle!" she cried, "when my father was
    slain,
What white man, who ravaged along that dread plain,
Withheld the dire blow, and plead for the life
Of Hillis-ad-joe? and say, who in that strife
Stayed the arm that bereft me, and left me alone?
Yes, Young Eagle! my father, my brothers are gone!
Wouldst thou ask me to linger behind them, while they
To yon heaven in the west are wending their way?
And, hark! the Great Spirit, whose voice sounds on
    high,
Bids me come! and see, white man, how gladly I
    fly!"
More swift than the deer, when the hounds are in
    view,
To the bark that was stranded, Chicomico flew!
She dashed the light oar in the waves' foaming spray
And thus wildly she sung, as she darted away :—

  "I go to the land in the west,
     The Great Spirit calls me away!
   To the land of the just and the blest,
     The Great Spirit points me the way!

  "Like snow on the mountain's crest,
    Like foam on the fountain's breast,
   Hillis-ad-joe and his kinsmen have passed!
    Like the sun's setting ray in the west,
    When it sinks on the wave to rest,
   The dead chieftain's daughter is coming at last!

" Too long has she lingered behind,
　　Awaiting the Great Spirit's voice !
But hark ! it calls loud in the wind,
　　And Chicomico now will rejoice !

" I go to the land in the west :
　　The Great Spirit calls me away !
To the land of the just and the blest,
　　The Great Spirit points me the way !"

The wild notes sunk upon the gale,
　　And echo caught them not again !
For the breeze which bore the maiden's wail,
　　Wafted afar the last sad strain !

'Twas said, that shrieking 'mid the storm,
　　The maiden oft was seen to glide,
And oft the hunters marked her form,
　　As swift she darted through the tide.

And once along the calm lake shore,
　　Her light canoe was she seen to guide,
But the maid and her bark are seen no more
　　To float along the rippling tide.

For the billows foamed, and the winds did roar,
　　And her lamp, as it glimmered amid the storm,
A moment blazed bright, and was seen no more,
　　For it sunk 'mid the waves with her maniac form !

THE FAREWELL.

Adieu, Chicomico, adieu ;
  Soft may'st thou sleep amid the wave,
And 'neath thy canopy of blue
  May sea-maids deck thy coral grave.

'Twas but a feeble voice which sung
  Thy hapless tale of youthful woe ;
But ah ! that weak, that infant tongue
  Will ne'er another story know.

And though the rough and foaming surge,
  And the wild whirlwind whistling o'er,
Should rudely chant thy funeral dirge,
  And send the notes from shore to shore ;

Still shall *one* voice be heard, above
  The dreadful " music of the spheres ! "
The voice of one whose song is love,
  Embalmed by sorrow's saddest tears.

PART V.

THE fourth day found the dark tribe brooding o'er
Their chieftain's body, chieftain now no more !
As fire half-quenched, some faint spark lives,
Glimmers, half dies, and then revives,

Revives to kindle far and wide,
And spread with devastating stride;
So glimmered, so revived, so spread
The mourners' rage around the dead!
Their quivers o'er their shoulders flung,
Up rose the aged and the young;
And swore, as tenants of the wood,
By all their hearts held dear or good,
That, ere another sun should rise,
Their slaughtered foes should glut their eyes.
They swore revenge and bloodshed too,
As their slain chieftain's rightful due;
They swore that blood should freely flow
For their poor, lost Chicomico!

'Twas evening: all was fair and still:
The orb of night now sparkling on the rill,
Now glittering o'er the fern, and water-brake,
Cast its broad eye-beam o'er the lake!
Far through the forest, where no foot-path lay,
Old Montonoe pursued his onward way;
The fair-haired stranger hung upon his arm,
Shook at each noise, and trembled with alarm;
" Well do I know the woodland way,
For I have tracked it many a day,
When mountain bear or wilder deer
Have called me to this forest drear.
Fear'st thou with Montonoe to stray,
Why wanderest thou so far away,
From friends, from safety, and from home,
To war, and weariness, and gloom?

Thou must not hope, as yet, to bear
Free from disguise that form so dear ;
It must not, and it will not be,
Till, buried in the dark Monce,
The last of yonder tribe of blood
Lies weltering in the sable flood !
But rest thee on this fresh green seat,
And I will trace his wandering feet ;
Warn him to watch the lurking foe,
Whose bloody breasts for vengeance glow ;
Then rest thee here ; within yon dell
I saw his form, and knew him well ?"

Thus spoke the prophet of the wood,
As near the stranger maid he stood.

" Then go," she cried, half faltering, "go !
Bid him beware the bloody foe !
But give me, ere we part," she cried,
" Yon blood-stained death-blade from your side ;
Perhaps this arm, though weak, may find
    Strength in the hour of deep distress ;
Go ! my preserver and my friend,
    May heaven thy steps and efforts bless !"

Cautious and swift the Indian went ;
His head was raised, his bow was bent,
And as he on, like wild deer, sped,
So light, so silent, was his tread,
That scarce a leaf was heard to move,
Of flower below, or branch above !

Where Rathmond, with a heart of woe,
Had gazed on lost Chicomico,
There, on that spot, the prophet's eye
Marked the young warrior's farewell sigh.

" Why lingerest thou here, Young Eagle," he cried,
" The foe 'neath the fern and the dark hazel hide !
Blood, blood ! be our war-cry, for vengeance is theirs !
Their arrows are winged by despair and by fears !
When the last of the tribe of Hillis-ad-joe
Hath plunged him beneath the deep waters below,
Thy heart shall possess all it wishes for here,
Unchilled by a sigh, unbedewed by a tear !
But till then, cold and vacant thy bosom shall be,
And the idol to which thou hast bended thy knee,
Shall mark thee, and love thee, in peril and woe,
Yet till then that dear being thou never shalt know !"

" What mean'st thou, prophet of the eagle-eye,
By thy mysterious prophecy ?
Well knowest thou that yon bloody chief
Doomed her to death, and me to grief !
That round that form the wild flames rolled
And wafted far her angel soul !
Why didst thou not arrest the brand ?
For, prophet, fate was in thy hand."

" 'Tis well," the Indian calmly said,
" 'Tis well," and bowed to earth his head ;
" But," he exclaimed, with eye less grave,
" I left a skiff on yonder wave —

Say, dark-eyed Eagle, dost thou know
Aught of the dire, blood-thirsty foe ? "

" No, Montonoe ! no foe was she,
Who plunged adown the swift Monee.
Chicomico is cold and damp !
The wave her couch — the moon her lamp ;
But mark ! adown the foaming stream
The barks beneath the moon's pale beam !
What bode they ? or of weal, or woe ?
Do they betoken friend or foe ?
Perchance to rouse the wildwood deer
The Indian hunters landed there."

Back they retraced their steps, till from the hill
A female shriek rang loud, distinct, and shrill !
Both start, both stop, and Montonoe's dark eye
Flashed like a meteor of the northern sky.
But hark ! what cry of savage joy is there,
Borne through the forest on the midnight air ?

It is the foe ! the band of blood-hounds came,
Who erst had lit the Chieftain's funeral flame !
Revenge and death around their arrows gleam,
And murder shudders 'neath the moon's pale beam !
The fiercest warrior of their tribe, their chief,
Sage in the council, bloody in the strife,
High towered dark Wompaw's snowy plume in air,
Waved on the breeze, and shone a beacon there !
Old Ompahaw, with brow of fire,
And bosom burning high with ire,

And sparkling eye, and burning brand,
Which gleamed athwart both lake and strand,
Still echoed back the lengthened yell
Which startled wildwood, rock and dell!
And more were there, so dread, so wild,
Nature might shudder at her child,
And curse the hand that e'er had made
So dark a stain, so deep a shade!

On, on they flew, with lengthened stride;
　　But, ah! the victims, where are they? —
Naught but the lake lies open wide,
　　And the broad bosom of the bay!
But, ah! 'tis well; that shrill shriek tolled
　　The death-knell of their chief once more!
Yes, Rathmond, yes, the deed was bold,
　　That stretched yon white plume on the shore!

Safe crouched 'neath fern-bush, dark and low,
Rathmond had truly bent his bow,
And Montonoe, with steady eye,
From 'mid the oak's arms, broad and high,
Took aim as sure; his arrows sped,
And many a bloody foe is dead!
Wide tumult spreads! afar they fly,
Each rustling brake, which meets the eye,
Seems shrouding still some warrior there,
With bloody brand and eye of fire.
Slow dropping from his safe retreat,
The prophet glides to Rathmond's seat;
Then raised loud yells of various tone,
Such as are given at victory won,

And Rathmond joined, till long and high,
Rang the loud chorus to the sky!
Hark! o'er the rocks, the shrieks are answered wild;
Can it be Echo, Nature's darling child?
No; 'tis a whoop of horror and despair,
Which knows no sympathy, which sheds no tear!

Lo! on yon cliff, which frowns above the wave,
Mark the stern warriors hovering o'er their grave!
'Tis done: the sullen bosom of the bay
Opens and closes o'er its sinking prey!

One hollow splashing, as the waters part,
    Sad welcome of the victim to his bed,
One mournful, shuddering echo, and the heart
    Turns, chilled, at length, from scenes of death and
        dread!

But, ah! like some sad spectre lingering near,
    A form still hovers o'er the scene of woe;
Does it await its hour of vengeance here,
    Watching the cold forms weltering below?

The morn was dawning slowly in the east,
    A few faint gleams of light were bursting through
When the dread warriors sought the lake's calm breast,
    And sullen sunk amid its waters blue!

That rude, wild phantom hovering there,
Poised on the precipice midway in air,
Like some stern spirit of the dead,
Rising indignant from its bed,
Was Ompahaw! alone, he stood,

Gazing on heaven, on hill, and wood!
His eye was wilder than the eagle's glare;
Its glance was triumph, mingled with despair!
Far floated on the breeze his plumes of red,
Waving in warlike pride around his head;
His bow was aimless, bent within his hand;
His scalping-knife was gleaming in its band;
And his gay dress, bedecked for battle's storm,
Was wildly fluttering round his warrior form!

" Farewell!" he cried, "this aged hand
Draws the last bow-string of our band!"
He spoke, and, sudden as the lightning's glance,
The dart, one moment, o'er the waters danced;
Like comet's blaze, like shooting star,
It whirled across the waters far!
The dark lake sparkled, as the arrow fell,
Foaming, death's herald, a last, bright farewell!
Then from his belt his tomahawk he tore,
" Man shall ne'er stain thy blade again with gore!"
Then raised on high his arm, and wildly sung
The death-song of his tribe, till Nature rung!

THE DEATH-SONG.

" The last of the tribe of Hillis-ad-joe
Falls not by the hand of the bloody foe;
But they fled to the heaven of peace in the west;
The Great Spirit called, and they flew to be blessed!

" From the dark rock's frowning brow
They flew to the deep below;

They feared not. for the heaven of peace in the west
Was smiling them welcome, sweet welcome to rest!

"The last of the tribe of Hillis-ad joe
Now plunges him 'mid the deep waters below!
I come, Great Spirit, take me to thy rest!
Lo! my freed soul is winged towards the west!"

'Tis past! the rude, wild sons of Nature sleep,
Calm, undisturbed, amid the waters deep!
'Tis past! the deed is done, the tribe has gone!
Not one is left to mourn it, no. not one!

The last of all that tribe of blood
Lies weltering in the sable flood!
O! where is yonder fair-haired maid?
Say, whither hath the lone one strayed?
'Mid the wild tumult of the strife,
Where fled she from the scalping-knife?
Angels around her spread their arm.
And shrouded her from fear and harm!
But oh, what shriek rang shrill and clear,
And echoed still in Rathmond's ear?
Why should he note that voice, that scream?
Was it his fancy, or a dream?
Or was it — hope illumed his eye,
And pointed to the prophecy!

"But no! — 'twere madness to return
   To those bright scenes of joy," he cried,
"Her bones are whitening in the sun,
   Her ashes scattered far and wide!"

But where is Montonoc? alone,
  Rathmond is musing on the strand;
Say, whither has the prophet gone?
  Why does young Rathmond heedless stand?

O! he is picturing to his vacant breast
Those scenes of joy, those moments doubly blessed,
Which youthful hope had promised should be his,
When all was light, and love, and cloudless bliss!
O! he was sighing o'er the dreary waste.
  Left in that bosom, which had loved so well!
O! he was wishing for some place of rest,
  Some gloomy cavern, or some lonely cell'

But, ah! the voice of Montonoc is heard,
Loud as the notes of yonder gloomy bird;
" Eagle!" he cried, " the fatal charm hath passed!
The blood-red tribe have darkly sunk at last!
And, warrior, now I yield unto thy power
The latest trophy of my life's last hour!
Deal with him as thou wilt, for he is thine!
But mark! 'twas I who gave, for he was mine!
Adieu! I go!" He closed his fiery eye,
And his stern spirit flew to heaven on high!

The prisoner sighed, and mutely gazed awhile
Upon the fallen prophet's brow of toil,
Then towards the warrior turned, dropped the dark
      hood,
And lo! Cordelia before Rathmond stood!
    1822.

MISCELLANEOUS PIECES.

—•—

AN ACROSTIC.

THE MOON.

Lo! yonder rides the empress of the night!
Unveiled she casts around her silver light;
Cease not, fair orb, thy slow majestic march,
Resume again thy seat in yon blue arch.
E'en *now*, as weary of the tedious way,
Thy head on Ocean's bosom thou dost lay;
In his blue waves thou hid'st thy shining face,
And gloomy darkness takes its vacant place.

THE SUN.

[IN CONTINUATION.]

Darting his rays the sun now glorious rides,
And from his path fell darkness quick divides;
Vapor dissolves and shrinks at his approach.
It dares not on his blazing path encroach;
Down droops the flow'ret, and his burning ray
Scorches the workmen o'er the new-mown hay.
O, lamp of Heaven, pursue thy glorious course,
Nor till gray twilight, aught abate thy force.

1819.

CHARITY.

A VERSIFICATION OF PART OF THE THIRTEENTH CHAPTER OF FIRST
CORINTHIANS.

THOUGH I were gifted with an angel's tongue,
And voice like that with which the prophets sung,
Yet if mild charity were not within,
'Twere all an impious mockery and sin.

Though I the gift of prophecy possessed,
And faith like that which Abraham professed,
They all were like a tinkling cymbal's sound,
If meek-eyed charity did not abound.

Though I to feed the poor my goods bestow,
And to the flames my body I should throw,
Yet the vain act would never cover sin
If heaven-born charity were not within.

    1820.

ON THE DEATH OF QUEEN CAROLINE.

Star of England! Brunswick's pride!
Thou hast suffered, drooped, and died!
Adversity, with piercing eye,
Bade all her arrows round thee fly ;
She marked thee from thy cradle-bed,
And plaited thorns around thy head! —
As the moon, whom sable clouds
Now brightly shows — now darkly shrouds —
So envy, with a serpent's eye,
And slander's tongue of blackest dye,
On thy pure name aspersions cast,
And triumphed o'er thy fame at last!
But each dark tale of guilt and shame
Shall darker fly to whence it came!
A stranger in a foreign land,
Oppressed beneath a tyrant's hand,
She drank the bitter cup of woe,
And read Fate's blackening volume through!
The last, the bitterest drop was drank,
The volume closed — and all was blank!

A HERO'S DUST.

And does a hero's dust lie here?
Columbia! gaze and drop a tear!
His country's and the orphan's friend,
See thousands o'er his ashes bend!

Among the heroes of the age,
He was the warrior and the sage!
He left a train of glory bright
Which never will be hid in night.

The toils of war and danger past,
He reaps a rich reward at last;
His pure soul mounts on cherub's wings,
And now with saints and angels sings.

The brightest on the list of fame
In golden letters shines his name;
Her trump shall sound it through the world,
And the striped banner ne'er be furled!

And every sex and every age,
From lisping boy to learned sage,
The widow and her orphan son,
Revere the name of WASHINGTON!

THE EVENING SPIRIT.

When the pale moon is shining bright,
And nought disturbs the gloom of night,
'Tis then upon yon level green,
From which St. Clair's dark heights are seen,
The Evening Spirit glides along,
And chants her melancholy song;
Or leans upon a snowy cloud,
And its white skirts her figure shroud.
By zephyrs light she's wafted far,
And contemplates the northern star,
Or gazes from her silvery throne,
On that pale queen, the silent moon.

Who is the Evening Spirit fair,
That hovers o'er thy walls, St. Clair?
Who is it, that with footstep light,
Breathes the calm silence of the night?
Ask the light zephyr who conveys
Her fairy figure o'er the waves;
Ask yon bright fleecy cloud of night,
Ask yon pale planet's silver light,
Why does the Evening Spirit fair
Sail o'er the walls of dark St. Clair?

TO SCIENCE.

Let others in false Pleasure's court be found,
But may I ne'er be whirled the giddy round ;
Let me ascend with Genius' rapid flight,
Till the fair hill of Science meets my sight.

Blest with a pilot who my feet will guide,
Direct my way, whene'er I step aside ;
May one bright ray of Science on me shine,
And be the gift of learning ever mine.

PLEASURE.

Away! unstable, fleeting Pleasure,
Thou troublesome and gilded treasure :
When the false jewel changes hue,
There's naught, O man, that's left for you!
What many grasp at with such joy,
Is but her shade, a foolish toy ;
She is not found at every court,
At every ball, and every sport,
But in that heart she loves to rest,
That's with a guiltless conscience blest.

THE GOOD SHEPHERD.

The shepherd feeds his fleecy flock with care,
   And mourns to find one little lamb has strayed;
He, unfatigued, roams through the midnight air,
   O'er hills, o'er rocks, and through the mossy glade.

But when that lamb is found, what joy is seen
   Depicted on the careful shepherd's face,
When, sporting o'er the smooth and level green,
   He sees his favorite charge is in its place.

Thus the great Shepherd of his flock doth mourn,
   When from his fold a wayward lamb has strayed,
And thus with mercy He receives him home,
   When the poor soul his Lord has disobeyed.

There is great joy among the saints in heaven,
   When one repentant soul has found its God,
For Christ, his Shepherd, hath his ransom given,
   And sealed it with his own redeeming blood!

4

LINES,

WRITTEN UNDER THE PROMISE OF REWARD.

WHENE'ER the Muse pleases to grace my dull page,
At the sight of *reward*, she flies off in a rage ;
Prayers, threats, and entreaties I frequently try,
But she leaves me to scribble, to fret, and to sigh.

She torments me each moment, and bids me go write,
And when I obey her, she laughs at the sight ;
The rhyme will not jingle, the verse has no sense,
And against all her insults I have no defense.

I advise all my friends, who wish me to write,
To keep their rewards and their praises from sight ;
So that jealous Miss Muse won't be wounded in pride,
Nor Pegasus rear, till I've taken my ride.

TO THE

MEMORY OF HENRY KIRKE WHITE.

In yon lone valley where the cypress spreads
Its gloomy, dark, impenetrable shades,
The mourning *Nine*, o'er White's untimely grave
Murmur their sighs, like Neptune's troubled wave.

There sits Consumption, sickly, pale, and thin,
Her joy evincing by a ghastly grin;
There his deserted garlands withering lie,
Like him they droop, like him untimely die.

STILLING THE WAVES.

"And He arose and rebuked the wind, and said unto the sea,
'Peace, be still!'"

Be still, ye waves, for Christ doth deign to tread
On the rough bosom of your watery bed!
Be not too harsh your gracious Lord to greet,
But, in soft murmurs, kiss his holy feet;
'Tis He alone can calm your rage at will,
This is his sacred mandate, "Peace, be still!"

A SONG.

(IN IMITATION OF THE SCOTCH.)

Wha is it that caemeth sae blithe and sae swift,
His bonnet is far frae his flaxen hair lift,
His dark een rolls gladsome, i' the breeze floats his
        plaid,
And surely he bringeth nae news that is sad.
Ah! say, bonny stranger, whence caemest thou now?
The tiny drop trickles frae off thy dark brow.

"I come," said the stranger, "to spier my lued hame,
And see if my Marion still were the same ;
I hae been to the battle, where thousands hae bled,
And chieftains fu' proud are wi' mean peasants laid ;
I hae fought for my country, for freedom, and fame,
And now I'm returning wi' speed to my hame."

"Gude Spirit of Light!" ('twas a voice caught his ear)
"And is it me ain Norman's accents I hear?
And has the fierce Southron then left me my child!
Or am I wi' sair, sair anxiety wild?"
He turned to behold — 'tis his mother he sees!
He flies to embrace her — he falls on his knees.

"O! where is my father?" a tear trickled down,
And silently moistened the warrior's cheek brown ;

'Ah! sure my heart sinks, sae sair in my breast,
Too sure he frae all the world's trouble doth rest!"
'But where is my Marion?" his pale cheek turned
      red,
And the glistening tear in his eye was soon dried.

'She lives!" and he knew 'twas his Marion's sweet
      tone,
'She lives," exclaims Marion, "for Norman alone!"
He saw her: the rose had fled far from her cheek,
But Norman still lives! his Marion is found;
By the adamant chains of blithe Hymen they're
      bound.

EXIT FROM EGYPTIAN BONDAGE.

When Israel's sons, from cruel bondage freed,
Fled to the land by righteous Heaven decreed;
Insulting Pharaoh quick pursued their train,
E'en to the borders of the troubled main.

Affrighted Israel stood alone dismayed,
The foe behind, the sea before them laid;
Around, the hosts of bloody Pharaoh fold,
And wave o'er wave the raging Red Sea rolled.

But God, who saves his chosen ones from harm,
Stretched to their aid his all-protecting arm,
And lo! on either side the sea divides,
And Israel's army in its bosom hides.

Safe to the shore through watery walls they march,
And once more hail kind Heaven's aerial arch;
Far, far behind, the cruel foe is seen,
And the dark waters roll their march between.

The God of vengeance stretched his arm again,
And heaving, back recoiled the foaming main;
And impious Pharaoh 'neath the raging wave,
With all his army, finds a watery grave.

Rejoice, O Israel! God is on your side,
He is your champion, and your faithful guide ;
By day, a cloud is to your footsteps given ;
By night, a fiery column towers to heaven.

Then Israel's children marched by day and night,
Till Sinai's mountain rose upon their sight :
There righteous Heaven the flying army stayed,
And Israel's sons the high command obeyed.

To Sinai's mount the trembling people came,
'Twas wrapped in threatening clouds, in smoke, and
    flame ;
A silent awe pervaded all the van ;
Not e'en a murmur through the army ran.

High Sinai shook! dread thunders rent the air!
And horrid lightnings round its summit glare !
'Twas God's pavilion, and the black'ning clouds,
Dark hovering o'er, his dazzling glory shrouds.

To Heaven's dread court the intrepid leader came,
To receive its mandate in the people's name ;
Loud trumpets peal — the awful thunders roll,
Transfixing terrors in each guilty soul.

But lo! He comes, arrayed in shining light,
And round his forehead plays a halo bright :
Heaven's high commands with trembling were re-
    ceived,
Heaven's high commands were heard, and were be-
    lieved.

THE LAST FLOWER OF THE GARDEN.

THE last flower of the garden was blooming alone ;
The last rays of the sun on its blushing leaves shone ;
Still a glittering drop on its bosom reclined,
And a few half-blown buds 'midst its leaves were en-
      twined.

Say, lonely one, say, why lingerest thou here ?
And why on thy bosom reclines the bright tear ?
'Tis the tear of a zephyr -- for summer 'twas shed,
And all thy companions now withered and dead.

Why lingerest thou here, when around thee are strown
The flowers once so lovely, by Autumn blast blown ?
Say, why, sweetest floweret, the last of thy race,
Why lingerest thou here the lone garden to grace ?

As I spoke, a rough blast, sent by Winter's own hand,
Whistled by me, and bent its sweet head to the sand ;
I hastened to raise it — the dew-drop had fled,
And the once lovely flower was withered and dead.

ODE TO FANCY.

Fancy, sweet and truant sprite,
Steals on wings, as feathers light,
Draws a veil o'er Reason's eye,
And bids the guardian senses fly.

Soft she whispers to the mind,
Come, and trouble leave behind :
She banishes the fiend Despair,
And shuts the eyes of waking Care.

Then, o'er precipices dark,
Where never reached the wing of lark,
Fearing no harm, she dauntless flies,
Where rocks on rocks dread frowning rise.

When Autumn shakes his hoary head,
And scatters leaves at every tread ;
Fancy stands with listening ear,
Nor starts, when shrieks affrighted Fear.

There's music in the rattling leaf,
But 'tis not for the ear of Grief;
There's music in the wind's hoarse moan,
But 'tis for Fancy's ear alone.

THE BLUSH.

Why that blush on Ella's cheek,
What doth the flitting wanderer seek?
Doth passion's blackening tempest scowl,
To agitate my Ella's soul?

Return, sweet wanderer, fear no harm;
The heart which Ella's breast doth warm,
Is virtue's calm, serene retreat:
And ne'er with passion's storm did beat.

Return, and calmly rest, till love
Shall thy sweet efficacy prove;
Then come, and thy loved place resume,
And fill that cheek with youthful bloom.

A blush of nature charms the heart
More than the brilliant tints of art;
They please awhile, and please no more, —
We hate the things we loved before.

But no unfading tints were those
Which to my Ella's cheek arose:
They please the raptured heart, and fly
Before they pall the gazing eye.

'Twas not the blush of guilt or shame
Which o'er my Ella's features came :
'Twas she who fed the poor distressed,
'Twas she the indigent had blessed ;

For her their prayers to heaven were raised,
On her the grateful people gazed ;
'Twas when the blush suffused her cheek,
Which told what words can never speak.

A SONG.

TUNE, — *Mrs. Robinson's Farewell.*

TELL me not of joys departed,
  Or of childhood's happy hour!
When unconsciously I sported,
  Fresh as morning's dewy flower!

Tell me not of fair hopes blasted,
  Or of unrequited love!
Tell me not of fortune wasted,
  Or the web which Fate hath wove!

One fond wish I long have cherished,
  I have twined it round my heart!
While all other hopes have perished,
  I with *that* could never part.

On life's troubled, stormy ocean
  That bright star still shone serene?
To *that* star, my heart's devotion
  Rose, at morning and at e'en!

And the hope that led me onward,
  Like a beacon shining bright,
Was — that when this form had mouldered,
  I might wake to realms of light!

Wake to bliss — that changes never !
　Wake no more to hope or fear !
Wake to joys that bloom forever,
　Withered by no sigh, no tear !

ON AN ÆOLIAN HARP.

WHAT heavenly music strikes my ravished ear,
So soft, so melancholy, and so clear?
And do the tuneful Nine then touch the lyre,
To fill each bosom with poetic fire?

Or does some angel strike the sounding strings,
Catching from echo the wild note he sings?
But hark! another strain, how sweet, how wild!
Now rising high, now sinking low and mild.

And tell me now, ye spirits of the wind,
O, tell me where those artless notes to find!
So lofty now, so loud, so sweet, so clear,
That even angels might delighted hear!

But hark! those notes again majestic rise,
As though some spirit, banished from the skies,
Had hither fled to charm Æolus wild,
And teach him other music sweet and mild.

Then hither fly, sweet mourner of the air,
Then hither fly, and to my harp repair;
At twilight chant the melancholy lay,
And charm the sorrows of thy soul away.

THE COQUETTE.

I HAE nae sleep, I hae nae rest,
    My Ellen's lost for aye,
My heart is sair and much distressed,
    I surely soon must die.

I canna think o' wark at a',
    My eyes still wander far,
I see her neck like driven snaw,
    I see her flaxen hair.

Sair, sair, I begged; she would na' hear,
    She proudly turned awa',
Unmoved she saw the trickling tear,
    Which, spite o' me, would fa'.

She acted weel a conqueror's part,
    She triumphed in my woe,
She gracefu' waved me to depart,
    I tried, but could na' go.

"Ah why," (distractedly I cried,)
    "Why yield me to despair?
Bid lingering Hope resume her sway,
    To ease my heart sae sair."

She scornfu' smiled, and bade me go!
   This roused my dormant pride ;
I craved nae boon — I took nae leuk,
   "Adieu!" I proudly cried.

I fled! nor Ellen hae I seen,
   Sin' that too fatal day :
My "bosom's laird" sits heavy here,
   And Hope's fled far away.

Care, darkly brooding, bodes a storm,
   I'm Sorrow's child indeed ;
She stamps her image on my form,
   I wear the mourning weed!

ON THE DEATH OF AN INFANT.

Sweet child, and hast thou gone, forever fled?
Low lies thy body in its grassy bed;
But thy freed soul swift bends its flight through air,
Thy heavenly Father's gracious love to share.

And now, methinks, I see thee clothed in white,
Mingling with saints, like thee, celestial bright.
Look down, sweet angel, on thy friends below,
And mark their trickling tears of silent woe.

Look down with pity in thy infant eye,
And view the friends thou left, for friends on high.
Methinks I see thee leaning from above,
To whisper, to those friends, of peace and love:

"Weep not for me, for I am happy still,
And murmur not at our great Father's will;
Let not this blow your trust in Jesus shake,
Our Saviour gave, and it is his to take.

"Once you looked forward to life's opening day,
The scene was bright, and pleasant seemed the way;
Hope drew the picture, Fancy, ever near,
Colored it bright — 'tis blotted with a tear.

5

"Then let that tear be Resignation's child ;
Yielding to Heaven's high will, be calm, be mild ;
Weep for your child no more, she's happy still,
And murmur not at your great Father's will."

REFLECTIONS,

ON CROSSING LAKE CHAMPLAIN IN THE STEAMBOAT "PHŒNIX."

Islet * on the lake's calm bosom,
  In thy breast rich treasures lie ;
Heroes ! there your bones shall moulder,
  But your fame shall never die.

Islet on the lake's calm bosom,
  Sleep serenely in thy bed ;
Brightest gem our waves can boast,
  Guardian angel of the dead !

Calm upon the waves recline,
  Till great Nature's reign is o'er ;
Until old and swift-winged time
  Sinks, and order is no more.

Then thy guardianship shall cease,
  Then shall rock thy aged bed ;
And when Heaven's last trump shall sound,
  Thou shalt yield thy noble dead !

* Crab Island ; on which were buried the remains of the sailors who fell in the action of September 11th, 1814.

THE STAR OF LIBERTY.

THERE shone a gem on England's crown,
   Bright as yon star;
Oppression marked it with a frown,
He sent his darkest spirit down,
To quench the light that round it shone,
   Blazing afar.
But Independence met the foe,
And laid the swift-winged demon low.

A second messenger was sent,
   Dark as the night;
On his dire errand swift he went,
But Valor's bow was truly bent,
Justice her keenest arrow lent,
   And sped its flight;
Then fell the impious wretch, and Death
Approached, to take his withering breath.

Valor then took, with hasty hand,
   The gem of light;
He flew to seek some other land,
He flew to 'scape oppression's hand,
He knew there was some other strand,
   More bright;
And as he swept the fields of air,
He found a country, rich and fair.

Upon its breast the star he placed,
　　　　　The star of liberty:
Bright, and more bright the meteor blazed,
The lesser planets stood amazed,
Astonished mortals, wondering, gazed,
　　　　　Looking on fearfully.
That star shines brightly to this day,
On thy calm breast, America!

ON SOLITUDE.

Sweet Solitude, I love thy silent shade !
   I love to pause when in life's mad career,
To view the checkered path before me laid,
   And turn to meditate — to hope, to fear.

'Tis sweet to draw the curtain on the world,
   To shut out all its tumult, all its care, —
Leave the dread vortex, in which all are whirled,
   And to thy shades of twilight calm repair.

Yet, Solitude, the hand divine, which made
   The earth, the ocean, and the realms of air,
Pointed how far thy kingdom should extend,
   And bade thee pause, for He had fixed thee there.

Then, when disgusted with the world and man,
   When sick of pageantry, of pomp, and pride,
To thee I'll fly, in thee I'll seek relief,
   And hope to find that calm the world denied.

THE DESTRUCTION OF SODOM AND GOMORRAH.

"And he looked towards Sodom and Gomorrah, and lo! the smoke of
the country went up as the smoke of a furnace."

O DREAD was the night, when o'er Sodom's wide plain
   The fire of heaven descended;
For all that then bloomed shall ne'er bloom there
      again,
   For man hath his Maker offended.

The midnight of terror and woe hath passed by,
   The death-spirit's pinions are furled;
But the sun, as it beams clear and brilliant on high,
   Hides from Sodom's dark, desolate world.

Here lies but that glassy, that death-stricken lake,
   As in mockery of what had been there;
The wild bird flies far from the dark nestling brake,
   Which waves its scorched arms in the air.

In that city the wine-cup was brilliantly flowing,
. Joy held her high festival there;
Not a fond bosom dreaming (in luxury glowing)
   Of the close of that night of despair.

For the bride, her handmaiden the garland was
  . wreathing,
  At the altar the bridegroom was waiting,
But vengeance impatiently round them was breathing,
  And death at that shrine was their greeting.

But the wine-cup is empty, and broken it lies,
  The lip which it foamed for, is cold ;
For the red wing of Death o'er Gomorrah now flies,
  And Sodom is wrapped in its fold.

The bride is wedded, but the bridegroom is Death,
  With his cold, damp, and grave-like hand ;
Her pillow is ashes, the slime-weed her wreath,
  Heaven's flames are her nuptial band.

And near to that cold, that desolate sea
  Whose fruits are to ashes now turned,
Not a fresh-blown flower, not a budding tree,
  Now blooms where those cities were burned.

THE WEE FLOWER OF THE HEATHER.

Thou pretty wee flower, humble thing,
    Thou brightest jewel of the heath,
Which waves at zephyr's lightest wing,
    And trembles at the softest breath ;

Thou lovely bud of Scotia's land,
    Thou pretty fragrant *burnie* gem,
By whispering breezes thou art fanned,
    And greenest leaves entwine thy stem.

No raging tempest beats thee down,
    Or finds thee in thy safe retreat ;
By no rough wintry winds thou'rt blown,
    Safe seated at the dark rock's feet.

ON READING A FRAGMENT CALLED "THE FLOWER OF THE FOREST."

Sing on, sweetest songster the woodland can boast;
    Sing on, for it charms, though it sorrows my breast;
The strains, though so mournful, shall never be lost,
    Till this throbbing bosom has murmured to rest.

The sweet Flower of the Forest on memory's page
    Shall bloom undecaying while life lingers near,
Unhurt by the storms which around it shall rage,
    By sorrow's sigh fanned, and bedewed by a tear.

TO MAMMA.

THE PARTING OF DECOURCY AND WILHELMINE.

Lo! enthroned on golden clouds,
  Sinks the monarch of the day ;
Now yon hill his glory shrouds,
  And his brilliance fades away.

But as it fled, one ling'ring beam
  Played o'er yon spire, which points on high ;
It cast one bright, one transient gleam,
  Then hastened from the deep'ning sky.

Lo! the red-tipped clouds remain
  But to tell of glories past ;
Mark them gathering o'er the plain,
  Mark them fade away at last.

The lake is calm, the breeze is still,
  Nor dares to whisper o'er a leaf ;
And nothing save the murm'ring rill,
  Can give the vacant ear relief.

Around yon hawthorn in the vale,
  White garments float like evening mist:
'Tis Wilhelmine; and cold and pale,
  A simple marble stone she kissed.

She knelt her by a lowly tomb,
  And wreathed its urn anew with flowers;
She taught the white rose there to bloom,
  And watered it with sorrow's showers.

Like raven's wing, her glossy hair
  In ringlets floated on the gale,
Or hung upon a brow as fair
  As snow-curl crested in the vale.

And her dark eye, which rolls so wild,
  Once brightly sparkled with hope's light,
For Wilhelmine was pleasure's child,
  When fortune's smiles shone sweetly bright.

.   .   .   .

Decourcy loved — the morn was clear,
  And fancy promised bliss;
For now the happy hour was near,
  Which made the maiden his.

And Wilhelmine sat smiling sweet
  Beneath the spreading tree;
Her nimble foot was quick to meet,
  Her glancing eye to see.

Decourcy came upon his steed,
  His brow and cheek were pale ;
" Speak — speak, Decourcy !" cried the maid,
  "'Tis sure a dreadful tale."

" My love, my Wilhelmine," cried he,
  " Be calm and fear thee not ;
In battle I will think on thee,
  And O, forget me not.

" Adieu !" he clasped her to his breast,
  And kissed the trickling tear
Which 'neath her half-closed eyelids prest
  And ling'ring glistened there.

He gazed upon that death-like face,
  So beautiful before ;
He gazed upon that shrine of grace,
  And dared to gaze no more.

He trembled, pressed his burning brow,
  And closed his aching eyes :
His limbs refuse their office now,
  The maid before him lies.

But hark ! the trumpet's warlike sound
  Echoes from hill to vale ;
He caught the maiden from the ground,
  And kissed her forehead pale.

Why should Decourcy linger there,
  When the bugle bids him speed ?

One long last look of calm despair,
  And he springs upon his steed ;

He strikes the sting of his bloody spur
  In his foaming courser's side,
And he gallops on where the wave of war
  Rolls on with its bursting tide.

Whose was the sword that flashed so bright,
  Like the flaming brand of heaven ?
And whose the plume, that from morn till night
  Was a star to the hopeless given ?

'Twas thine, Decourcy ! that terrible sword
  Hath finished its work of death ;
But the hand which raised it on high is lowered
  To the damp green earth beneath.

The sun went down, and its parting ray
  Smiled sorrow across the earth,
The light breeze moaned — then died away,
  And the stars rose up in mirth.

And the timid moon looked down with a smile
  On the blood-stained battle ground,
And the groans of the wounded rose up the while
  With a sad, heart-rending sound, —

While the spectre-form of some grief-worn man
  Steals slowly and silently by,
Each corpse to note — each face to scan,
  For his friend on that field doth lie.

But whose is the figure dimly seen
  By the trembling moonbeam's light ?
'Tis the form of the weeping Wilhelmine,
  And she kneels by the slaughtered knight.

Weep not for the dead, for he died 'mid the din,
  And the rapturous shouts of strife,
And the bright sword hath ushered his soul within
  The portals of future life.

Weep not for the dead ! who would not die
  As that gallant soldier died ?
With a field of glory whereon to lie,
  And his foeman dead beside.

A year passed by, and a simple tomb
  Rose up 'neath a willow tree ;
'Twas decked with flowers in vernal bloom
  As fresh as flowers could be ;

And oft as the twilight's dusky gleam
  O'er the scene was gently stealing,
The form of the sorrowful maid was seen
  By the grave of her lover kneeling.

But wild is the glance of her dove-like eye,
  And her cheek, O how pale and fair
And the mingled smile, and the deep-drawn sigh,
  Show that reason's no longer there.

Another year passed, and another grave
　'Neath the willow tree is seen ;
By the side of her lover, Decourcy the brave,
　Lay the corpse of Wilhelmine.

AN ADDRESS TO MY MUSE.

Why, gentle Muse, wilt thou disdain
 To lend thy strains to me?
Why do I supplicate in vain
 And bow my heart to thee?

O! teach me how to touch the lyre,
 To tune the trembling chord ;
Teach me to fill each heart with fire,
 And melting strains afford.

Sweep but thy hand across the string,
 The woodlands echo round,
And mortals wond'ring, as you sing,
 Delighted catch each sound.

Enchanted when thy voice I hear,
 I drop each earthly care ;
I feel as wafted from the world
 To Fancy's realms of air.

Then as I wander, plaintive sing,
 And teach me every strain ;
Teach me to touch the trembling string
 Which now I strike in vain.

6

THE MERMAID.

MAID of the briny wave and raven lock,
Whose bed's the sea-weed, and whose throne's the rock,
Tell me, what fate compels thee thus to ride
O'er the tempestuous ocean's foaming tide?

Art thou some naiad, who, at Neptune's nod,
Flies to obey the mandate of that god?
Art thou the siren, who, when night draws on,
Chantest thy farewell to the setting sun?

Or, leaning on thy wave-encircled rock,
Twining with lily hand thy raven lock,
Dost thou, in accents wild, proclaim the storm
Which soon shall wrap the unwary sailor's form?

Or dost thou round the wild Charybdis play,
To warn the seaman from his dangerous way?
Or, shrieking midst the tempest, chant the dirge
Of shipwrecked sailors, buried in the surge?

Tell me, mysterious being, what you are?
So wild, so strange, so lonely, yet so fair!
Tell me, O tell me, why you sit alone,
Singing so sweetly on the wave-washed stone?

And tell me, that if e'er I find my grave
Beneath the ocean's wildly troubled wave,
That thou with weeds wilt strew my watery bed,
And hush the roaring billows o'er my head.

1823.

ON THE BIRTH OF A SISTER.

Sweet babe, I cannot hope thou wilt be freed
From woes, to all since earliest time decreed;
But mayest thou be with resignation blessed,
To bear each evil, howsoe'er distressed.

May Hope her anchor lend amid the storm,
And o'er the tempest rear her angel form!
May sweet Benevolence, whose words are peace,
To the rude whirlwinds softly whisper, "Cease!"

And may Religion, Heaven's own darling child,
Teach thee at human cares and griefs to smile;
Teach thee to look beyond this world of woe,
To Heaven's high fount, whence mercies ever flow.

And when this vale of tears is safely passed,
When Death's dark curtain shuts the scene at last,
May thy freed spirit leave this earthly sod,
And fly to seek the bosom of thy God.

A DREAM.

METHOUGHT (unwitting how the place I gained)
I rested on a fleecy, floating cloud
Far o'er the earth, the stars, the sun, the heavens,
And slowly wheeled around the dread expanse!
Sudden, methought, a trumpet's voice was heard,
Pealing with long, loud, death-awakening note,
Such note as mortal man but once may hear!
At that heart-piercing summons, there arose
A crowd fast pouring from the troubled earth!
The *earth*, that blackened speck, alone seemed moved
By the dread note, which rushed,
Like pent-up whirlwinds, round Heaven's azure vault;
All other worlds, all other twinkling stars
Stood mute — stood motionless ;
Their time had not yet come.
Yet, ever and anon, they seemed to bow
Before the dread tribunal ;
And the fiery comet, as it blazed along,
Stopped in its midway course, as conscious of the
    power
Which onward ever, ever had impelled :
No other planet moved, none seemed convulsed,
Save the dim orb of earth!
Forth eddying rushed a crowd, confused and dark,
Like a volcano, muttering and subdued !
There came no sound distinct, but sighs and groans

And murmurings half suppressed, half uttered!
All eyes were upward turned in wonder and in fear,
But soon, methought, they onward rolled
To the dread High One's bar,
As the tumultuous billows rush murmuring to the
　　　shore,
And all distinctions dwindled into naught.
Upward I cast my eyes ;
High on an azure throne, begirt with clouds,
Sate the dread Indescribable!
He raised his sceptre, waved it o'er the crowd,
And all was calm and silent as the grave !
He rose ; the cherubs flapped their snowy wings !
On came the rushing wind — the throne was moved,
And flew like gliding swan above the crowd!
Sudden it stopped o'er the devoted world !
The Judge moved forward 'mid his sable shroud,
Raised his strong arm with rolling thunders clothed,
Held forth a vial filled with wrathful fire,
Then poured the contents on the waiting globe!
Sudden the chain, which bound it to God's throne,
Snapped with a dire explosion !
On wheeled the desolate — the burning orb
Swift through the heavens !
Down, down it plunged; then shot across the expanse,
Blazing through realms where light had never pierced!
Down, down it plunged, fast wheeling from above,
Shooting forth flames, and sparks, and burning brands,
Trailing from shade to shade
Then bounding, blazing brighter than before,
It plunged extinguished in the chaotic gulf!

TO MY SISTER.

WHEN evening spreads her shades around,
  And darkness fills the arch of heaven;
When not a murmur, not a sound
  To Fancy's sportive ear is given;

When the broad orb of heaven is bright,
  And looks around with golden eye;
When Nature, softened by her light,
  Seems calmly, solemnly to lie;

Then, when our thoughts are raised above
  This world, and all this world can give,
O sister, sing the song I love,
  And tears of gratitude receive.

The song which thrills my bosom's core,
  And, hovering, trembles, half afraid;
O sister, sing the song *once* more
  Which ne'er for mortal ear was made.

'Twere almost sacrilege to sing
  Those notes amid the glare of day;
Notes borne by angels' purest wing,
  And wafted by their breath away.

When sleeping in my grass-grown bed,
   Shouldst thou *still* linger here above,
Wilt thou not kneel beside my head,
   And, sister, sing the song I love ?

CUPID'S BOWER.

Am I in fairy-land ? or tell me, pray,
To what love-lighted bower I've found my way?
Sure luckless wight was never more beguiled
In woodland maze, or closely tangled wild.

And is this Cupid's realm ? if so, good-by !
Cupid, and Cupid's votaries, I fly ;
No offering to his altar do I bring,
No bleeding heart — or hymeneal ring.

What though he proudly marshals his array
Of conquered hearts, still bleeding in his way,
Of sighs, of kisses sweet, of glances sly,
Playing around some darkly beauteous eye?

What though the rose of beauty, opening wide,
Blooms but for him, and fans his lordly pride?
What though his garden boasts the fairest flower
That ever dew-drop kissed, or pearly shower?

Still, Cupid, I'm no votary to thee ;
Thy torch of light will never blaze for me ;
I ask no glance of thine, I ask no sigh ;
I brave thy fury, and thus boldly fly !

Adieu, then, and for evermore, adieu !
Ye poor entangled ones, farewell to you!
And, O ye powers ! a hapless mortal prays
For guidance through this labyrinthine maze.

THE FAMILY TIME-PIECE.

Friend of my heart, thou monitor of youth,
Well do I love thee, dearest child of truth,
Though many a lonely hour thy whisperings low
Have made sad chorus to the notes of woe.

Or 'mid the happy hour which joyful flew,
Thou still wert faithful, still unchanged, still true ;
Or when the task employed my infant mind,
Oft have I sighed to see thee lag behind ;

And watched thy finger, with a youthful glee,
When it had pointed, silently, "Be free:"
Thou wert my mentor through each passing year ;
'Mid pain or pleasure, thou wert ever near.

And when the wings of time unnoticed flew,
I paused, reflected, wondered, turned to you ;
Paused in my heedless round, to mark thy hand,
Pointing to conscience, like a magic wand ;

To watch thee stealing on thy silent way,
Silent, but sure, time's pinions cannot stay ;
How many hours of pleasure, hours of pain,
When smiles were bright'ning round affliction's train ?

How many hours of poverty and woe,
Which taught cold drops of agony to flow ?

How many hours of war, of blood, of death,
Which added laurels to the victor's wreath?

How many deep-drawn sighs thy hand hath told,
And dimmed the smile, and dried the tear which
    rolled
When the loud cannon spoke the voice of war,
And death and bloodshed whirled their crimson car?

When the proud banner, waving in the breeze,
Had welcomed war, and bade adieu to peace,
Thy faithful finger traced the wing of time,
Pointed to earth, and then to heaven sublime.

Unmoved amid the carnage of the world,
When thousands to eternity were hurled,
Thy head was reared aloft, truth's chosen child,
Beaming serenely through the troubled wild.

Friend of my youth, ere from its mould'ring clay
My joyful spirit wings to heaven its way,
O may'st thou watch beside my aching head,
And tell how fast time flits with feathered tread.

ON THE

EXECUTION OF MARY QUEEN OF SCOTS.

Touch not the heart, for Sorrow's voice
    Will mingle in the chorus wild;
When Scotland weeps, canst thou rejoice?
    No: rather mourn her murdered child.

Sing how on Carberry's mount of blood,
    'Mid foes exulting in her doom,
The captive Mary fearless stood,
    A helpless victim for the tomb.

Justice and Mercy, 'frighted, fled,
    And shrouded was Hope's beacon blaze,
When, like a lamb to slaughter led,
    Poor Mary met her murderers' gaze.

Calm was her eye as yon dark lake,
    And changed her once angelic form;
No sigh was heard the pause to break,
    That awful pause before the storm.

O draw the veil, 'twere shame to gaze
    Upon the bloody tragedy;
But lo! a brilliant halo plays
    Around the hill of Carberry.

'Tis done — and Mary's soul has flown
  Beyond this scene of blood and death ;
'Tis done — the lovely saint has gone
  To claim in heaven a thornless wreath.

But as Elijah, when his car
  Wheeled on towards heaven its path of light,
Dropped on his friend, he left afar,
  His mantle, like a meteor bright ;

So Mary, when her spirit flew
  Far from this world, so sad, so weary,
A crown of fame immortal threw
  Around the brow of Carberry.

RUTH'S ANSWER TO NAOMI.

Entreat me not, I must not hear;
Mark but this sorrow-beaming tear;
Thy answer's written deeply now
On this warm cheek and clouded brow;
'Tis gleaming o'er this eye of sadness,
Which only near *thee* sparkles gladness.

The hearts *most* dear to us are gone,
And *thou* and *I* are left alone;
Where'er thou wanderest, I will go,
I'll follow thee through joy or woe;
Shouldst thou to other countries fly,
Where'er thou lodgest, there will I.

Thy people shall my people be,
And to thy God I'll bend the knee;
Whither thou fliest, will I fly,
And where thou diest, I will die;
And the same sod which pillows thee
Shall freshly, sweetly bloom for me.

DAVID AND JONATHAN.

On the brow of Gilboa is war's bloody stain, —
The pride and the beauty of Israel is slain!
O publish it not in proud Askelon's street,
Nor tell it in Gath, lest in triumph they meet,
              For how are the mighty fallen!

O mount of Gilboa, no dew shalt thou see,
Save the blood of the Philistine fall upon thee;
For the strong-pinioned eagle of Israel is dead;
Thy brow is his pillow, thy bosom his bed!
              O how are the mighty fallen!

Weep, daughters of Israel, weep o'er his grave!
What breast will now pity, what arm will now save?
O my brother! my brother! this heart bleeds for thee,
For thou wert a friend and a brother to me!
              Ah, how are the mighty fallen!

THE SICK-BED.

O HAVE you watched beside the bed,
Where rests the weary, aching head?
And have you heard the long, deep groan,
The low-said prayer, in half-breathed tone?

O have you seen the fevered sleep,
    Which speaks of agony within?
The eye which would, but cannot weep,
    And wipe away the stains of sin?

O have you marked the struggling breath,
    Which would but cannot leave its clay?
And have you marked the hand of death
    Unbind, and bid it haste away?

Then thou hast seen what thou shalt feel;
    Then thou hast read thy future doom;
O pause, one moment, o'er death's seal;
    There's no repentance in the tomb.

BYRON.

His faults were great, his virtues less,
  His mind a burning lamp of heaven ;
His talents were bestowed to bless,
  But were as vainly lost as given.

His was a harp of heavenly sound,
  The numbers wild, and bold, and clear ;
But ah ! some demon, hovering round,
  Tuned its sweet chords to Sin and Fear.

His was a mind of giant mould,
  Which grasped at all beneath the skies ;
And his a heart, so icy cold,
  That virtue in its recess dies.
    1823.

7

THE BACHELOR.

To the world (whose dread laugh he would tremble
    to hear,
From whose scorn he would shrink with a cowardly
    fear)
The old bachelor proudly and boldly will say,
Single lives are the longest, single lives are most gay.

To the ladies, with pride, he will always declare,
That the links in love's chain are strife, trouble, and
    care ;
That a wife is a torment, and he will have none,
But at pleasure will roam through the wide world
    alone.

And let him pass on, in his sulky of state ;
O say, who would envy that mortal his fate ?
To brave all the ills of life's tempest alone,
Not a heart to respond the warm notes of his own.

His joys undivided no longer will please ;
The warm tide of his heart through inaction will
    freeze :
His sorrows concealed, and unanswered his sighs,
The old bachelor curses his folly, and dies.

Pass on, then, proud lone one, pass on to thy fate ;
Thy sentence is sealed, thy repentance too late ;
Like an arrow, which leaves not a trace on the wind,
No mark of thy pathway shall linger behind.

Not a sweet voice shall murmur its sighs o'er thy
    tomb ;
Not a fair hand shall teach thy lone pillow to bloom ;
Not a kind tear shall water thy dark, lonely bed :
By the living 'twas scorned, 'tis refused to the dead.

ON THE CREW OF A VESSEL

WHO WERE FOUND DEAD AT SEA.

THE breeze blew fair, the waving sea
   Curled sparkling round the vessel's side ;
The canvas spread with bosom free
   Its swan-like pinions o'er the tide.

Evening had gemmed with glittering stars
   Her coronet so darkly grand ;
The Queen of Night, with fleecy clouds,
   Had formed her turban's snowy band.

On, on the stately vessel flew,
   With streamer waving far and wide ;
When lo ! a bark appeared in view,
   And gayly danced upon the tide.

Each way the breeze its wild wing veered,
   That way the stranger vessel turned ;
Now near she drew, now wafted far,
   She fluttered, trembled, and returned.

"It is the pirates' cursed bark !
   The villains linger to decoy !
Thus bounding o'er the waters dark,
   They seek to lure, and then destroy.

" Perchance those strange and wayward signs
    May be the signals of distress,"
The Captain cried, "for mark ye, now,
    Her sails are flapping wide and loose."

And now the stranger, vessel came
    Near to that gay and gallant bark;
It seemed a wanderer far and lone,
    Upon life's wave, so deep and dark.

And not a murmur, not a sound,
    Came from that lone and dreary ship;
The icy chains of silence bound
    Each rayless eye and pallid lip.

For Death's wing had been waving there,
    The cold dew hung on every brow,
And sparkled there like angel tears,
    Shed o'er the silent crew below.

Onward that ship was gayly flying,
    Its bosom was the sailor's grave;
The breeze 'mid the shrouds, in low notes, sighing
    Their requiem over the brave.

Fly on, fly on, thou lone vessel of death,
    Fly on with thy desolate crew;
For mermaids are twining a sea-weed wreath,
    'Mong the red coral groves for you.

WOMAN'S LOVE.

They told me of her history. Her love
Was a neglected flame, which had consumed
The vase wherein it kindled. O how fraught
With bitterness is unrequited love!
To know that we have cast life's hope away
On a vain shadow!
Hers was a gentle passion, quiet, deep,
As a woman's love should be,
All tenderness and silence, only known
By the soft meaning of a downcast eye,
Which almost fears to look its timid thoughts;
A sigh, scarce heard; a blush, scarce visible,
Alone may give it utterance. Love is
A beautiful feeling in a woman's heart,
When felt as only woman love *can* feel!
Pure as the snow-fall, when its latest shower
Sinks on spring-flowers; deep as a cave-locked foun-
        tain;
And changeless as the cypress's green leaves,
And like them, sad! She nourished
Fond hopes and sweet anxieties, and fed
A passion unconfessed, till he she loved
Was wedded to another. Then she grew
Moody and melancholy; one alone
Had power to soothe her in her wanderings, —
Her gentle sister; but that sister died,

And the unhappy girl was left alone,
A *maniac.* She would wander far, and shunned
Her own accustomed dwelling; and her haunt
Was that dead sister's grave: and that to her
Was as a home.

TO A LADY,

O! touch the chord yet once again,
   Nor chide me, though I weep the while ;
Believe me, that deep seraph strain
   Bore with it memory's moonlight smile.

It murmured of an absent friend ;
   . The voice, the air, 'twas all her own ;
And hers those wild, sweet notes which blend
   In one mild, murmuring, touching tone.

And days and months have darkly passed,
   Since last I listened to her lay ;
And Sorrow's cloud its shade hath cast,
   Since then, across my weary way.

Yet still the strain comes sweet and clear,
   Like seraph-whispers, lightly breathed ;
Hush, busy memory, Sorrow's tear
   Will blight the garland thou hast wreathed.

'Tis sweet, though sad — yes, I will stay,
I cannot tear myself away.

I thank thee, lady, for the strain ;
   The tempest of my soul is still ;
Then touch the chord yet once again,
   For thou canst calm the storm at will !

ON SEEING

A PICTURE OF THE BLESSED VIRGIN MARY,

PAINTED SEVERAL CENTURIES SINCE.

A FRAGMENT.

ROLL back, thou tide of time, and tell
Of book, of rosary, and bell ;
Of cloistered nun, with brow of gloom,
Immured within her living tomb ;
Of monks, of saints, and vesper-song,
Borne gently by the breeze along ;
Of deep-toned organ's pealing swell ;
Of Ave Marie, and funeral knell ;
Of midnight taper, dim and small,
Just glimmering through the high-arched hall ;
Of gloomy cell, of penance lone,
Which can for darkest deeds atone :
Roll back, and lift the veil of night.
For I would view the anchorite.
Yes, there he sits, so sad, so pale,
Shuddering at Superstition's tale :
Crossing his breast with meagre hand,
While saints and priests, a motley band,
Arrayed before him, urge their claim
To heal in the Redeemer's name ;

To mount the saintly ladder (made
By every monk, of every grade,
From portly abbot, fat and fair,
To yon lean starveling, shivering there),
And mounting thus, to usher in
The soul, thus ransomed from its sin.
And tell me, hapless bigot, why,
For what, for whom did Jesus die,
If pyramids of saints must rise
To form a passage to the skies?
And think you man can wipe away
With fast and penance, day by day,
One single sin, too dark to fade
Before a bleeding Saviour's shade?
O ye of little faith, beware!
For neither shrift, nor saint, nor prayer,
Will aught avail ye without Him
Beside whom saints themselves grow dim.
Roll back, thou tide of time, and raise
The faded forms of other days!
Yon time-worn picture, darkly grand,
The work of some forgotten hand,
Will teach thee half thy mazy way,
While Fancy's watch-fires dimly play;
Roll back, thou tide of time, and tell
Of secret charm, of holy spell,
Of Superstition's midnight rite,
Of wild Devotion's seraph flight.
Of Melancholy's tearful eye,
Of the sad votaress' frequent sigh,
That trembling from her bosom rose,
Divided 'twixt her Saviour's woes

And some warm image lingering there,
Which, half-repulsed by midnight prayer,
Still, like an outcast child, will creep
Where sweetly it was wont to sleep,
And mingle its unhallowed sigh
With cloister-prayer and rosary ;
Then tell the pale deluded one
Her vows are breathed to God alone :
Those vows, which tremulously rise,
Love's last, love's sweetest sacrifice.

       [*Unfinished.*]

AMERICAN POETRY.

A FRAGMENT.

MUST every shore ring boldly to the voice
Of sweet poetic harmony, save this?
Rouse thee, America! for shame! for shame!
  Gather thy infant bands, and rise to join
Thy glimmering taper to the holy flame:
  Such honor, if no other, may be thine.
Shall Gallia's children sing beneath the yoke?
  Shall Ireland's harp-strings thrill, though all un-
     strung?
And must America, her bondage broke,
  Oppression's blood-stains from her garment wrung,
Must she be silent? Who may then rejoice?
  If she be tuneless, Harmony, farewell!
O! shame, America! wild Freedom's voice
  Echoes, "shame on thee," from her wild-wood dell.
Shall conquered Greece still sing her glories past?
Shall humbled Italy in ruins smile?
And canst thou then —[*Unfinished.*]

HEADACHE.

Headache! thou bane to Pleasure's fairy spell,
Thou fiend, thou foe to joy, I know thee well!
Beneath thy lash I've writhed for many an hour, —
I hate thee, for I've known and dread thy power.

Even the heathen gods were made to feel
The aching torments which thy hand can deal;
And Jove, the ideal king of heaven and earth,
Owned thy dread power, which called stern Wisdom
        forth.

Wouldst thou thus ever bless each aching head,
And bid Minerva make the brain her bed,
Blessings might then be taught to rise from woe,
And Wisdom spring from every throbbing brow.

But always the reverse to me, unkind,
Folly forever dogs thee close behind;
And from this burning brow, her cap and bell,
Forever jingle Wisdom's funeral knell.

TO A STAR.

Thou brightly glittering star of even,
Thou gem upon the brow of heaven,
O! were this fluttering spirit free,
How quick 'twould spread its wings to thee.

How calmly, brightly dost thou shine,
Like the pure lamp in Virtue's shrine!
Sure the fair world which thou mayst boast
Was never ransomed, never lost.

There, beings pure as heaven's own air,
Their hopes, their joys, together share;
While hovering angels touch the string,
And seraphs spread the sheltering wing.

There cloudless days and brilliant nights,
Illumed by heaven's refulgent lights;
There seasons, years, unnoticed roll,
And unregretted by the soul.

Thou little sparkling star of even,
Thou gem upon an azure heaven,
How swiftly will I soar to thee,
When this imprisoned soul is free!

SONG OF VICTORY,

ON THE DEATH OF GOLIATH.

STRIKE with joy the wild harp's string,
God, O Israel, is your King!
We have slain our deadliest foe,
David's arm hath laid him low.

Saul hath oft his thousands slain,
His trophies have bedecked the plain ;
But David's tens of thousands lie
In slaughtered millions, mounted high.

Sound the trumpet — strike the string,
Loud let the song of victory ring ;
Wreathe with glory David's brow,
He hath laid Goliath low.

Mark him on yon crimson plain ;
He is conquered — he is slain ;
He who lately rose so high,
Scoffed at man, and braved the sky.

Strike with joy the wild harp's string,
God, O Israel, is your King!
We have slain our deadliest foe,
David's arm hath laid him low.

THE INDIAN CHIEF AND CONCONAY.

THE Indian Chieftain is far away,
  Through the forest his footsteps fly ;
But his heart is behind him with Conconay,
He thinks of his love in the bloody fray,
  When the storm of war is high.

But little he thinks of the bloody foe
  Who is bearing that love away ;
And little he thinks of her bosom's woe,
And little he thinks of the burning brow
  Of his lovely Conconay.

They tore her away from her friends, from her home,
  They tore her away from her Chief ;
Through the wild-wood, when weary, they forced her
      to roam,
Or to dash the light oar in the river's white foam,
  While her bosom o'erflowed with grief.

But there came a foot, 'twas swift, 'twas light,
  'Twas the brother of him she loved ;
His heart was kind, and his eye was bright ;
He paused not by day, and he slept not by night,
  While through the wild forest he roved.

8

'Twas Lightfoot, the generous, 'twas Lightfoot the
    young,
  And he loved the sweet Conconay ;
But his bosom to honor and virtue was strung,
And the chords of his heart should to breaking be
    wrung
  Ere love should gain o'er him the sway.

Far, far from her stern foes he bore her away,
  And sought his own forest once more ;
But sad was the heart of the young Conconay,
Her bosom recoiled when she strove to be gay,
  And was even more drear than before.

'Tis evening, and weary, and faint, and weak
  Is the beautiful Conconay ;
She could wander no farther, she strove to speak,
But lifeless she sunk upon Lightfoot's neck,
  And seemed breathing her soul away.

The young warrior raised his eyes to heaven,
  He turned them towards the west ;
For one moment a ray of light was given,
Like lightning, which through the cloud hath riven,
  But to strike at the fated breast.

For there was his brother returning from far,
  O'er his shoulder his scalps were slung ;
For he had been victor amid the war,
His plume had gleamed like the polar star,
  And on him had the victory hung.

The Chieftain paused in his swift career,
  For he knew his Conconay ;
He saw the maid his heart held dear,
On his brother's breast, in the forest drear,
  From her home so far away.

He bent his bow, the arrow flew,
  It was aimed at Lightfoot's breast ;
And it pierced a heart as warm and true
As ever a mortal bosom knew,
  Or in mortal garb was dressed.

He turned to his love — from her brilliant eye
  The cloud was passing away ;
She let fall a tear — she breathed a sigh —
She turned towards Lightfoot — she uttered a cry,
  For weltering in gore he lay.

Her heart was filled with horror and woe,
  When she gazed on the form of her Chief ;
'Twas his loved hand that had bent the bow,
'Twas he who had laid her preserver low ;
  And she yielded her soul to grief.

And 'twas said, that ere time had healed the wound
  In the breast of the mourning maid,
That a pillar was reared on the fatal ground,
And ivy the snow-white monument crowned
  With its dark and jealous shade.

THE MOTHER'S LAMENT FOR HER INFANT.

Cold is his brow, and the dew of the evening
  Hangs damp o'er that form I so fondly caressed;
Dim is that eye which once sparkled with gladness;
  Hushed are the griefs of my infant at rest.

Calmly he lies on a bosom far colder
  Than that which once pillowed his health-blushing
    cheek;
Calmly he'll rest there, and silently moulder,
  No grief to disturb him, no sigh to awake.

Dread king of the grave, O! return me my child!
  Unfetter his heart from the cold chains of death!
Monarch of terrors, so gloomy, so silent,
  Loose the adamant clasp of thy cold, icy wreath!

Where is my infant? the storms may descend,
  The snows of the winter may cover his head;
The wing of the wind o'er his low couch may bend,
  And the frosts of the night sparkle bright o'er the
    dead.

Where is my infant? the damp ground is cold,
  Too cold for those features so laughing and light;
Methinks these fond arms should encircle his form,
  And shield off the tempest which wanders at night.

This fond bosom loved him, ah! loved him too dearly,
  And the frail idol fell, while I bent to adore ;
All its beauty has faded, and broken before me
  Is the god my heart ventured to worship before.

'Tis just, and I bow 'neath the mandate of Heaven ;
  Thy will, O my Father, forever be done!
Bless God, O my soul, for the chastisement given,
  Henceforth will I worship my Saviour alone!

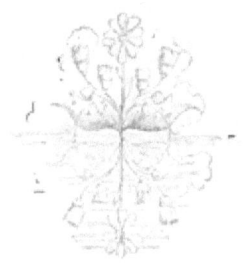

ON THE MOTTO OF A SEAL.

"IF I LOSE THEE, I AM LOST."

ADDRESSED TO A FRIEND.

WAFTED o'er a treacherous sea,
Far from home, and far from thee,
Between the heaven and ocean tossed,
"If I lose thee, I am lost."

When the polar star is beaming,
O'er the dark-browed billows gleaming,
I think of thee and dangers crossed,
For "If I lose thee, I am lost."

When the light-house fire is blazing,
High towards heaven its red crust raising,
I think of thee, while onward tossed,
For "If I lose thee, I am lost."

SHAKESPEARE.

Shakespeare! "with all thy faults (and few have
    more)
I love thee still," and still will con thee o'er.
Heaven, in compassion to man's erring heart,
Gave thee of virtue, then of vice a part,
Lest we, in wonder here, should bow before thee,
Break God's commandment, worship, and adore thee:
But admiration now. and sorrow join ;
His works we reverence, while we pity thine.

TO A LADY RECOVERING FROM SICKNESS.

THERE is a charm in the pallid cheek,
A charm which the tongue can never speak,
When the hand of sickness has withered awhile,
The rose which had bloomed in the rays of a smile.

There is a charm in the heavy eye,
When the tear of sorrow is passing by,
Like a summer shower o'er yon vault of blue,
Or the violet trembling 'neath drops of dew.

It spreads around a shade as light
As daylight blending with the night ;
Or 'tis like the tints of an evening sky,
And soft as the breathing of sorrow's sigh.

THE VISION.

'Twas evening — all was calm and silent, save
The low, hoarse dashing of the distant wave ;
The whip-poor-will had closed his pensive lay,
Which sweetly mourned the sun's declining ray ;
Tired of a world surcharged with pain and woe,
Weary of heartless forms and all below,
Broken each tie, bereft of every friend,
Whose sympathy might consolation lend,
And musing on each vain and earthly toy,
Walked the once gay and still brave Oleroy.
Thus lost in thought, unconsciously he strayed,
When a dark forest wild around him laid.
In vain he tried the beaten path to gain,
He sought it earnestly, but sought in vain ;
At length o'ercome, he sunk upon the ground,
Where the dark ivy twined its branches round :
Sudden there rose upon his wandering ear,
Notes which e'en angels might delighted hear.
Now low they murmur, now majestic rise,
As though "some spirit banished from the skies"
Had there repaired to tune the mournful lay,
"And chase the sorrows of his soul away."
They ceased — when lo ! a brilliant dazzling light
Illumed the wood and chased the shades of night ;
He raised his head ; there stood, near Oleroy,
The beauteous figure of a smiling boy ;

Across his shoulder hung an ivory horn,
With jewels glittering like the rays of morn;
In his white hand he held the tuneful lyre,
And in his eyes there beamed a heavenly fire;
Approaching Oleroy, he smiling cried, —
You hate the world and all its charms deride,
You hate the world and all it doth contain,
Condemn each joy, and call each pleasure pain;
Then come, he sweetly cried, come, follow me,
Another world thy sorrowing eyes shall see.

No sooner said than swift the smiling boy
Led from the bower the wond'ring Oleroy.
Beneath a tree three sylph-like forms recline;
Each form was beauteous, and each face benign;
Beside them stood a chariot dazzling bright,
Yoked with two beauteous swans of purest white;
They mount the chariot, and ascend on high;
They bend the lash, on wingéd winds they fly;
Above the spacious globe they stretch their flight;
That globe seemed now but as a cloud of night.
Swift towards the moon the white swans bend their
      way,
And a new world its treasures doth display.
They halt; before them rocks and hills are spread,
And birds, and beasts, which at their footsteps fled.
Another moon emits a softer ray,
And other moonbeams on the waters play:
They wander on, and reach a darksome cave,
Against whose side loud roars the dashing wave:
These words upon its rugged front appear, —

"What in your world is lost, is treasured here."
They enter; round upon the floor are strewn
The ivory sceptre, and the glittering crown;
Unnumbered hopes there fluttered on the wing,
There were the lays discarded lovers sing;
There Fame her trumpet blew, long, loud, and clear;
Worlds tremble as the deafening notes they hear;
There brooded riches o'er his lifeless heap;
There were the tears which misery's children weep;
There were posthumous alms, and misspent time
Lost in a jingling mass of foolish rhyme.
There was the conscience of the miser; there
The tears of love, — the pity of the fair;
There, pointing. cried the sylph-like smiling boy,
There's the *content* which fled you, Oleroy!
Regain it if you can; then far away,
And reach your world before the dawn of day.

ON SEEING AT A CONCERT THE PUBLIC PERFORMANCE OF A FEMALE DWARF.

HELPLESS, unprotected, weary,
  Tossed upon the world's wide sea,
Borne from those I love most dearly,
  Say — dost thou not feel for me?

Who that hath shrunk 'neath Nature's frown,
  Would court false fortune's fickle smile?
O, who would wander thus alone,
  Reckless alike of care or toil?

Who would, for fading pleasure, brave
  The sea of troubles, dark and deep?
For lo! the gems which deck the wave
  Vanish, and "leave the wretch to weep."

'Twas not for fortune's smile of light,
  Which beams but to destroy forever;
'Twas not for pleasure's bubbles bright,
  Which dazzle still, deluding ever:

Oft have I faltered when alone
  Before the crowd I sung my lay;
But ah, a father's feeble moan
  Rung in my ears, I dared not stay.

O, I have borne pride's scornful look,
  And burning taunts from slander's tongue ;
Yet more of malice I could brook,
  E'en though my heart with grief was wrung.

Adieu ! a long — a last adieu —
  Once more I launch upon life's sea ;
But still shall memory turn to you,
  For, stranger, you have felt for me.

ALONZO AND IMANEL.

As he spoke, he beheld on the sea-beaten strand
  A form, 'twas so airy, so light,
He could almost have sworn by the faith of his land
That an angel was wand'ring 'mid rocks and through
     sand,
  'Neath the moonbeam so fitfully bright.

He paused, as the bittern screamed loud o'er his head :
  One moment he paused on the shore,
To mark the wild wave as it dashed from its bed,
Tossing high the white spray from its foam-spangled
     head,
  With a fitful and deafening roar.

He caught the wild notes of a song, on the wind,
  Ere the tempest-god bore them away :
And they told of a tortured and desperate mind,
To despair's dark shadows forever resigned,
  Of a heart once hope-lighted and gay.

The bright moon was hid in the breast of the storm,
  And darkness and terror drew round ;
Yet still he could mark her light, fanciful form,
As she roamed round the wild rocks, devoid of alarm,
  Though the fiend of the whirlwind frowned.

O tell me, he cried, what spirit so light,
  So beautiful e'en in despair,
Is wand'ring alone 'mid the storm of the night,
When to guide her no star in the heaven is bright,
  No gleam save the lightning's red glare!

'Tis young Imanel, answered his guide with a sigh,
  The rich, the beloved, and the gay,
Who is doomed from her friends and her country to
      fly,
For she loved, and she wedded Alonzo the spy,
  Who has left her and fled far away.

Alonzo the spy! and he darted away
  With the speed of a shooting star,
Nor heeded the call of his guide to stay,
But toward the poor lone one he bounded away;
  She had fled to the sea-beach afar.

One glance of the forked lightning's glare
  Played bright round the fair one's face,
And it beamed on Alonzo, for he was there,
And it beamed on his bride, on his Imanel dear,
  Clasped at length in his joyful embrace.

TO MARGARET'S EYE.

O! I have seen the blush of morn,
　And I have seen the evening sky;
But ah! they faded when I gazed
　On the bright heaven of Margaret's eye.

I've seen the Queen of evening ride
　Majestic 'mid the clouds on high;
But e'en Diana in her pride
　Was dim near Margaret's brilliant eye.

I've seen the azure vault of heaven,
　I've seen the star-bespangled sky;
But O! I would the whole have given
　For one sweet glance from Margaret's eye.

I've seen the dew upon the rose;
　It trembled 'neath the zephyr's sigh;
But O! the tear which Nature shed
　Was dim near that in Margaret's eye.

A SONG.

LIFE is but a troubled ocean,
  Hope a meteor, love a flower
Which blossoms in the morning beam,
  And withers with the evening hour.

Ambition is a dizzy height,
  And glory but a lightning gleam ;
Fame is a bubble, dazzling bright,
  Which fairest shines in fortune's beam.

When clouds and darkness veil the skies,
  And sorrow's blast blows loud and chill,
Friendship shall like a rainbow rise,
  And softly whisper — " Peace, be still."

9

TWILIGHT.

How sweet the hour when daylight blends
   With the pensive shadows on evening's breast!
And dear to the heart is the pleasure it lends;
   'Tis like the departure of saints to their rest.

O, 'tis sweet, Saranac, on thy loved banks to stray,
   To watch the last day-beam dance light on thy
      wave,
To mark the white skiff as it skims o'er the bay,*
   Or heedlessly bounds o'er the warrior's grave.

O, 'tis sweet to a heart unentangled and light,
   When with hope's brilliant prospects the fancy is
      blest,
To pause 'mid its day-dreams so witchingly bright,
   And mark the last sunbeams, while sinking to rest.

    * Cumberland Bay, the scene of a battle during the last war.

THE WHITE MAID OF THE ROCK.

LOUD 'gainst the rocks the wild spray is dashing,
Its snowy white foam o'er the waves rudely splash-
    ing ;
The woods echo round to the bittern's shrill scream,
As he dips his black wing in the wave of the stream ;
Now mournful and sad the low murmuring breeze
Sighs lonely and dismal through hollow oak trees.
The owl loudly hoots, while his lonely abode
Serves to shelter the snake and the poisonous toad ;
Lo! the black thunder-cloud is spread over the skies,
And the swift-winged lightning at intervals flies.
The streamlet looks dark, and the spray wilder breaks ;
And the alder-leaf dank with its silver drop, shakes ;
This dell and these rocks, this lone alder and stream,
With the dew-drops which dance in the moon's silver
    beam,
Are sacred to beings ethereal and light,
Who hold their dark orgies alone and at night.
Wild, and more wild, dashed the waves of the stream,
The White Maid of the Rock gave a shrill, piercing
    scream ;
Down headlong she plunged 'neath the dark rolling
    wave,
And, rising, thus chanted a dirge to the brave : —
" The raven croaks loud from her nest in the rock,
The night-owl's shrill hooting resounds from the oak ;

Behold the retreat where brave Avenel is laid,
Uncoffined, except by his own Scottish plaid!
Long since has my girdle diminished to naught,
And the great house of Avenel low has been brought;
The star now burns dimly which once brightly shone,
And proud Avenel's glory forever has flown.
As I sailed and my white garments caught in the
  brake,
'Neath the oak, whose huge branches extend o'er the
  lake,
'Woe to thee! woe to thee! Maid of the Rock,'
Cried the night-raven who builds in the oak;
'Woe to thee! guardian spirit of Avenel!
Where are thy holly-bush, streamlet, and dell?
No longer thou sittest to watch and to weep,
Near the abbey's lone walls, and its turrets so steep!
Woe to thee! woe to thee! Maid of the Rock,'
Cried the night-raven who builds in the oak!
Then farewell, great Avenel, thy proud race is run!
The girdle has vanished — my task is now done."
Then her long flowing tresses around her she drew,
And her form 'neath the wave of the dark streamlet
  threw.

HABAKKUK III. 6.

WHEN Cushan was mourning in solitude drear,
When the curtains of Midian trembled with fear,
On the wings of salvation thy chariot did fly:
Thou didst stride the wide whirlwind and come from
      on high.

Earth shook, and before thee the mountains did bow:
The voice of the deep thundered loud from below ;
Thy arrows glanced bright as they shot through the
      air,
And far gleamed the light of thy glittering spear ;
The bright orb of day paused in wonder on high,
And the lamp of the night stood still in the sky.

LOVE, JOY, AND PLEASURE.

AN ALLEGORY.

THE night was calm, the sky serene,
  The sea a mirror displayed;
On its bosom the twinkling stars were seen,
The moon-crested waves were dancing between,
  And smiling through evening's shade.

On that placid sea Pleasure's bark was riding,
  Love and Joy were its guides through the deep;
And their hearts beat high, while on fortune con-
    fiding,
They smiled at the forms that were gloomily striding
  O'er the brow of the wave-washed steep.

Those forms were Malice, and Scorn, and Hate,
  And they flitted around so dark,
That they seemed like the gloomy sisters of Fate,
Intent on some dreary, some deadly debate,
  To ruin the beautiful bark.

But the eye of Joy was raised on high,
  She gazed at the moon's pale lamp;
The tear of pleasure shone bright in her eye,
And she saw not the clouds that were passing by,
  Death's messengers dark and damp.

And Pleasure was gazing with childish glee
  At the beacon's trembling gleam.
Or watching the shade of her wings in the sea,
With their colors as varied and fickle as she,
  As fleeting as Folly's dream.

And Love was tipping his feathery darts,
  And feeding his flaming torch ;
He was tinging his wings with the blood of hearts ;
He was chanting low numbers, and smiling by starts
  At the flowers round Hymen's porch.

Meanwhile the clouds were gath'ring drear,
  They hung round the weeping moon,
And still the mariners dreamed not of fear,
Still in Joy's bright eye beamed the brilliant tear,
  Which sorrow would claim too soon.

The voice of the tempest-god rolled around,
  The bark towards heaven was tossed ;
Then, then the fond dreamers awoke at the sound,
And Pleasure, the helmsman, in agony found
  That the light-house fire was lost.

Loud and more loud the billows roar,
  The ocean no more is gay ;
Love dreams of his pinions and arrows no more,
Joy mourns the hour that she left the shore,
  And Pleasure's bright wings fade away.

Then Malice sent forth a shadowy bark,
　　Which, bounding o'er the wave,
Came like a meteor's brilliant spark,
A star of light mid the tempest dark,
　　A beacon of hope from the grave.

Joy onward rushed to the airy skiff
　　Which near them gayly drew;
But ah! she sank to the arms of Grief,
For the bark, which promised them sure relief,
　　Away like lightning flew.

Then the smile of Scorn and Malice gleamed
　　Across the billow's foam,
And long and loud fell Hatred screamed
With fiend-like joy, as the lightning streamed
　　Around their forms of gloom.

On, on, they drifted before the gale ;
　　Again the signal rose ;
Joy and Pleasure the beacon hail ;
Love's ashy cheek becomes less pale
　　As clearer and brighter it glows.

'Twas Hope who fired the beacon high,
　　And she came with her anchor of rest ;
And Faith, who raised towards heaven her eye,
Spoke peace to the storm of the troubled sky,
　　And calm to the weary breast.

And Charity came with her robe of light,
  And she led the wanderers home ;
She warned them and wept o'er the woes of the
      night,
And she welcomed them in with a smile so bright,
  That Pleasure forgot to roam.

And she led them to Religion's shrine,
  Where Hope was humbly kneeling,
And *there* the tears of Joy did shine
With a light more dazzling, more divine, —
  They were mingled with tears of feeling.

There Love's wild wings shone calmly bright,
  As over the altar he waved them ;
There Pleasure folded her pinions light,
And fondly gazed with a sacred delight
  On the scroll which Charity gave them.

O THAT THE EAGLE'S WING WERE MINE!

O THAT the eagle's wing were mine!
  I'd soar above the dreary earth ;
I'd spread my wings, and rise to join
  The immortal fountain of my birth.

For what is joy? how soon it fades, —
  The childish vision of an hour!
Though warm and brilliant are its shades,
  'Tis but a frail and fading flower.

And what is hope? it is a light
  Which leads us on deluding ever,
Till lost amid the shades of night
  We sink, and then it flies forever!

And what is love? it is a dream,
  A brilliant fable framed by youth ;
A bubble dancing on life's stream,
  And sinking 'neath the eye of truth.

And what are honor, glory, fame,
  But Death's dark watchwords to the grave?
The victim dies, and lo! his name
  Is lost in life's swift rolling wave.

And what are all the joys of life,
  But vanity, and toil, and woe?
What but a bitter cup of grief,
  With dregs of sin and death below?

This world is but the first dark gate
  Unfolded to the waking soul;
But Death unerring, led by Fate,
  Shall heaven's bright portals backward roll.

Then shall this unchained spirit fly
  On to the God who gave it life;
Rejoicing as it soars on high,
  Released from danger, doubt, and strife.

There will it pour its anthems forth,
  Bending before its Maker's throne, —
The great I Am, who gave it birth,
  The Almighty God, the dread Unknown.

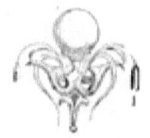

THE SMILE OF INNOCENCE.

THERE is a smile of bitter scorn,
    Which curls the lip, which lights the eye;
There is a smile in beauty's morn,
    Just rising o'er the midnight sky.

There is a smile of youthful joy,
    When Hope's bright star 's the transient guest;
There is a smile of placid age,
    Like sunset on the billow's breast.

There is a smile, the maniac's smile,
    Which lights the void which reason leaves,
And, like the sunshine through a cloud,
    Throws shadows o'er the song she weaves.

There is a smile of love, of hope,
    Which shines a meteor through life's gloom;
And there's a smile, Religion's smile,
    Which lights the weary to the tomb.

There is a smile, an angel's smile,
    That sainted souls behind them leave;
There is a smile that shines through toil,
    And warms the bosom though in grief;

And there's a smile on Nature's face,
　When Evening spreads her shades around ;
A pensive smile when twinkling stars
　Are glimmering through the vast profound.

But there's a smile, 'tis sweeter still,
　'Tis one far dearer to my soul ;
It is a smile which angels might
　Upon their brightest list enroll.

It is the smile of innocence,
　Of sleeping infancy's light dream ;
Like lightning on a summer's eve,
　It sheds a soft and pensive gleam.

It dances round the dimpled cheek,
　And tells of happiness within ;
It smiles what it can never speak, —
　A human heart devoid of sin.

TO MY MOTHER.

O thou whose care sustained my infant years,
   And taught my prattling lip each note of love ;
Whose soothing voice breathed comfort to my fears,
   And round my brow hope's brightest garland wove :

To thee my lay is due, the simple song
   Which Nature gave me at life's opening day ;
To thee these rude, these untaught strains belong,
   Whose heart indulgent will not spurn my lay.

O say, amid this wilderness of life,
   What bosom would have throbbed like thine for me?
Who would have smiled responsive ? who in grief
   Would e'er have felt, and, feeling, grieved like thee?

Who would have guarded, with a falcon eye,
   Each trembling footstep or each sport of fear?
Who would have marked my bosom bounding high,
   And clasped me to her heart, with love's bright tear?

Who would have hung around my sleepless couch,
   And fanned, with anxious hand, my burning brow?
Who would have fondly pressed my fevered lip,
   In all the agony of love and woe?

None but a mother, —none but one like thee,
　Whose bloom has faded in the midnight watch ;
Whose eye, for me, has lost its witchery,
　Whose form has felt disease's mildew touch.

Yes, thou hast lighted me to health and life,
　By the bright lustre of thy youthful bloom ;
Yes, thou hast wept so oft o'er every grief,
　That woe hath traced thy brow with marks of
　　gloom.

O then, to thee this rude and simple song,
　Which breathes of thankfulness and love for thee,
To thee, my mother, shall this lay belong,
　Whose life is spent in toil and care for me.

SABRINA.

A VOLCANIC ISLAND, WHICH APPEARED AND DISAPPEARED AMONG
THE AZORES, IN 1711.

ISLE of the ocean, say, whence comest thou?
The smoke thy dark throne, and the blaze round thy
     brow;
The voice of the earthquake proclaims thee abroad,
And the deep, at thy coming, rolls darkly and loud.

From the breast of the ocean, the bed of the wave,
Thou hast burst into being, hast sprung from the
     grave;
A stranger, wild, gloomy, yet terribly bright,
Thou art clothed with the darkness, yet crowned with
     the light.

Thou comest in flames, thou hast risen in fire;
The wave is thy pillow, the tempest thy choir;
They will lull thee to sleep on the ocean's broad breast,
A slumbering volcano, an earthquake at rest.

Thou hast looked on the isle — thou hast looked on
     the wave—
Then hie thee again to thy deep, watery grave;
Go, quench thee in ocean, thou dark, nameless thing,
Thou spark from the *fallen one's* wide flaming wing.

THE PROPHECY.

LET me gaze awhile on that marble brow,
On that full, dark eye, on that cheek's warm glow ;
Let me gaze for a moment, that, ere I die,
I may read thee, maiden, a prophecy.
That brow may beam in glory awhile ;
That cheek may bloom, and that lip may smile ;
That full dark eye may brightly beam
In life's gay morn, in hope's young dream ;
But clouds shall darken that brow of snow,
And sorrow blight thy bosom's glow.
I know by that spirit so haughty and high,
I know by that brightly flashing eye,
That, maiden, there's that within thy breast.
Which hath marked thee out for a soul unblest :
The strife of love with pride shall wring
Thy youthful bosom's tenderest string ;
And the cup of sorrow, mingled for thee,
Shall be drained to the dregs in agony.
Yes, maiden, yes, I read in thine eye
A dark and a doubtful prophecy.
Thou shalt love, and that love shall be thy curse :
Thou wilt need no heavier, thou shalt feel no worse.
I see the cloud and the tempest near ;
The voice of the troubled tide I hear ;

10

The torrent of sorrow, the sea of grief,
The rushing waves of a wretched life.
Thy bosom's bark on the surge I see,
And, maiden, thy loved one is there with thee.
Not a star in the heavens, not a light on the wave!
Maiden, I've gazed on thine early grave.
When I am cold, and the hand of Death
Hath crowned my brow with an icy wreath,
When the dew hangs damp on this motionless lip,
When this eye is closed in its long last sleep,
Then, maiden, pause, when thy heart beats high,
And think on my last sad prophecy.

PROPHECY II.

I HAVE told a maiden of hours of grief,
Of a bleeding heart, of a joyless life ;
I have read her a tale of future woe ;
I have marked her a pathway of sorrow below ;
I have read on the page of her blooming cheek
A darker doom than my tongue dare speak.
Now, maiden, for thee, I will turn mine eye
To a brighter path through futurity.
The clouds shall pass from thy brow away,
And bright be the closing of life's long day ;
The storms shall murmur in silence to sleep,
And angels around thee their watches shall keep.
Thou shalt live in the sunbeams of love and delight,
And thy life shall flow on till it fades into night ;
And the twilight of age shall come quietly on ;
Thou wilt feel, yet regret not, that daylight hath
        flown :
For the shadows of evening shall melt o'er thy soul,
And the soft dreams of heaven around thee shall roll,
Till sinking in sweet, dreamless slumber to rest,
In the arms of thy loved one, still blessing and blest,
Thy soul shall glide on to its harbor in heaven,
Every tear wiped away, every error forgiven.

PROPHECY III.

WILT thou rashly unveil the dark volume of fate?
It is open before thee: repentance is late, —
Too late! for, behold o'er the dark page of woe
Move the days of thy grief, yet unnumbered below.
There is one whose sad destiny mingles with thine:
He was formed to be happy — he dared to repine;
And jealousy mixed in his bright cup of bliss,
And the page of his fate grew still darker than this.
He gazed on thee, maiden, he met thee, and passed;
But better for thee had the Siroc's fell blast
Swept by thee, and wasted and faded thee there,
So youthful, so happy, so thoughtless, so fair.
And mark ye his broad brow? 'tis noble; 'tis high;
And mark ye the flash of his dark, eagle-eye?
When the wide wheels of time have encircled the
      world,
When the banners of night in the sky are unfurled,
Then, maiden, remember the tale I have told,
For further I may not, I dare not unfold.
The rose on yon dark page is sear and decayed,
And thus, e'en in youth, shall thy fondest hopes fade;
Tis an emblem of thee, broken, withered, and pale —
Nay, start not, and blanch not, though dark be the
      tale:

An hour-glass half spent, and a tear-bedewed token,
A heart withered, wasted, and bleeding and broken,
All these are the emblems of sorrow to be ;
I will veil the page, maiden, in pity to thee.

FEATS OF DEATH.

I HAVE passed o'er the earth in the darkness of night,
I have walked the wild winds in the morning's broad
  light ;
I have paused o'er the bower where the infant lay
  sleeping,
And I've left the fond mother in sorrow and weeping.

My pinion was spread, and the cold dew of night,
Which withers and moulders the flower in its light,
Fell silently o'er the warm cheek in its glow,
And I left it there blighted, and wasted, and low ;
I culled the fair bud, as it danced in its mirth,
And I left it to moulder and fade on the earth.

I paused o'er the valley ; the glad sounds of joy
Rose soft through the mist, and ascended on high ;
The fairest were there, and I paused in my flight,
And the deep cry of wailing broke wildly that night.

I stay not to gather the lone one to earth,
I spare not the young in their gay dance of mirth,
But I sweep them all on to their home in the grave ;
I stop not to pity — I stay not to save.

I paused in my pathway, for beauty was there :
It was beauty too death-like, too cold, and too fair !

The deep purple fountain seemed melting away,
And the faint pulse of life scarce remembered to play;
She had thought on the tomb, she was waiting for me:
I gazed, I passed on, and her spirit was free.

The clear stream rolled gladly, and bounded along,
With ripple, and murmur, and sparkle, and song;
The minstrel was tuning his wild harp to love,
And sweet and half sad were the numbers he wove.
I passed, and the harp of the bard was unstrung;
O'er the stream which rolled deeply, 'twas recklessly
      hung:
The minstrel was not! and I passed on alone,
O'er the newly raised turf and the rudely carved
      stone.

AUCTION EXTRAORDINARY.

I DREAMED a dream in the midst of my slumbers,
And as fast as I dreamed it, it came into numbers;
My thoughts ran along in such beautiful metre,
I'm sure I ne'er saw any poetry sweeter.
It seemed that a law had been recently made
That a tax on old bachelors' pates should be laid;
And in order to make them all willing to marry,
The tax was as large as a man could well carry.
The bachelors grumbled, and said 'twas no use;
'Twas horrid injustice and horrid abuse;
And declared that, to save their own hearts'-blood
      from spilling,
Of such a vile tax they would not pay a shilling.
But the rulers determined *them* still to pursue,
So they set the old bachelors up at vendue.
A crier was sent through the town to and fro,
To rattle his bell, and his trumpet to blow,
And to call out to all he might meet in his way,
" Ho! forty old bachelors sold here to-day!"
And presently all the old maids in the town,
Each in her very best bonnet and gown,
From thirty to sixty, fair, plain, red, and pale,
Of every description, all flocked to the sale:
The auctioneer then in his labor began,
And called out aloud, as he held up a man,

"How much for a bachelor? who wants to buy?"
In a twink,* every maiden responded, "I, — I;"
In short, at a highly extravagant price,
The bachelors all were sold off in a trice;
And forty old maidens, some younger, some older,
Each lugged an old bachelor home on her shoulder.

* "That in a *twink* she won me to her love." — *Shakespeare.* — [ED.]

THE "GUARDIAN ANGEL."

TO MISS E. C.—COMPOSED ON A BLANK LEAF OF HER "PALEY,"
DURING RECITATION.

I'm thy guardian angel, sweet maid, and I rest
In mine own chosen temple, thy innocent breast;
At midnight I steal from my sacred retreat,
When the chords of thy heart in soft unison beat.

When thy bright eye is closed, when thy dark tresses
        flow
In beautiful wreaths o'er thy pillow of snow,
O then I watch o'er thee, all pure as thou art,
And listen to music which steals from thy heart.

Thy smile is the sunshine which gladdens my soul,
My tempest the clouds which around thee may roll;
I feast my light form on thy rapture-breathed sighs,
And drink at the fount of those beautiful eyes.

The thoughts of thy heart are recorded by me;
There are some which, half breathed, half acknowl-
        edged by thee,
Steal sweetly and silently o'er thy pure breast,
Just ruffling its calmness, then murmuring to rest.

Like a breeze o'er the lake, when it breathlessly lies,
With its own mimic mountains, and star-spangled
        skies,

I stretch my light pinions around thee when sleeping,
To guard thee from spirits of sorrow and weeping.

I breathe o'er thy slumbers sweet dreams of delight,
Till you wake but to sigh for the visions of night.
Then remember, wherever your pathway may lie,
Be it clouded with sorrow, or brilliant with joy,
My spirit shall watch thee, wherever thou art,
My incense shall rise from the throne of thy heart.
Farewell! for the shadows of evening are fled,
And the young rays of morning are wreathed round
        my head.

TO THE VERMONT CADETS.

Pass on! for the bright torch of glory is beaming;
 Go, wreathe round your brows the green laurels
  of fame;
Around you a halo is brilliantly streaming,
 And history lingers to write down each name.

Yes! ye are the pillars of liberty's throne;
 When around you the banner of glory shall wave,
America proudly shall claim you her own,
 And freedom and honor shall pause o'er each grave!

A watch-fire of glory, a beacon of light,
 Shall guide you to honor, shall point you to fame:
The heart that shrinks back, be it buried in night,
 And withered with dim tears of sorrow and shame!

Though death should await you, 'twere glorious to die
 With the glow of pure honor still warm on the brow;
With a light sparkling brightly around the dim eye,
 Like the smile of a spirit still ling'ring below.

Pass on, and when War in his strength shall arise,
 Rush on to the conflict, and conquer or die;
Let the clash of your arms proudly roll to the skies:
 Be blest if victorious — and cursed, if you fly!

TO MY FRIEND AND PATRON.

M—— K——, ESQ.

And can my simple harp be strung
  To higher theme, to nobler end,
Than that of gratitude to thee,
  To thee, my father and my friend?

I may not, cannot, will not say
  All that a grateful heart would breathe;
But I may frame a simple lay,
  Nor Slander blight the blushing wreath.

Yes, I will touch the string to thee,
  Nor fear its wildness will offend;
For well I know that thou wilt be
  What thou hast ever been, — a friend.

There are, whose cold and idle gaze
  Would freeze the current where it flows;
But Gratitude shall guard the fount,
  And Faith shall light it as it flows.

Then tell me, may I dare to twine,
  While o'er my simple harp I bend,
This little offering for thee,
  For thee, my father and my friend?

MORNING.

I COME in the breath of the wakened breeze;
I kiss the flowers, and I bend the trees;
And I shake the dew which hath fallen by night,
From its throne on the lily's pure bosom of white.
Awake thee, when bright from my couch in the sky
I beam o'er the mountains, and come from on high;
When my gay purple banners are waving afar;
When my herald, gray dawn, hath extinguished each
    star;
When I smile on the woodlands, and bend o'er the
    lake,
Then awake thee, O maiden, I bid thee awake!
Thou mayst slumber when all the wide arches of
    heaven
Glitter bright with the beautiful fire of even;
When the moon walks in glory, and looks from on
    high,
O'er the clouds floating far through the clear azure
    sky,
Drifting on like the beautiful vessels of heaven,
To their far-away harbor all silently driven,
Bearing on, in their bosoms, the children of light,
Who have fled from this dark world of sorrow and
    night;
When the lake lies in calmness and darkness, save
    where
The bright ripple curls, 'neath the smile of a star;

When all is in silence and solitude here,
Then sleep, maiden, sleep! without sorrow or fear!
But when I steal silently over the lake,
Awake thee then, maiden, awake! O, awake!

TO A FRIEND,

AND thou hast marked, in childhood's hour,
　The fearless boundings of my breast,
When, fresh as Summer's opening flower,
　I freely frolicked, and was blessed.

O! say, was not this eye more bright?
　Were not these lips more wont to smile?
Methinks that then my heart was light,
　And I a fearless, joyous child.

And thou didst mark me gay and wild,
　My careless, reckless laugh of mirth;
The simple pleasure of a child,
　The holiday of man on earth.

Then thou hast seen me in that hour
　When every nerve of life was new,
When pleasures fanned youth's infant flower,
　And Hope her witcheries round it threw.

That hour is fading, — it has fled,
　And I am left in darkness now;
A wanderer towards a lowly bed,
　The grave, that home of all below.

MODESTY.

THERE is a sweet, though humble flower,
  Which grows in nature's wildest bed ;
It blossoms in the lonely bower,
  But withers 'neath the gazer's tread.

'Tis reared alone, far, far away
  From the wild noxious weeds of death ;
Around its brow the sunbeams play,
  The evening dew-drop is its wreath.

'Tis Modesty ; 'tis Nature's child ;
  The loveliest, sweetest, meekest flower
That ever blossomed in the wild,
  Or trembled 'neath the evening shower.

'Tis Modesty ; so pure, so fair,
  That woman's witcheries lovelier grow,
When that sweet flower is blooming there,
  The brightest beauty of her brow.

11

THE YELLOW FEVER.

THE sky is pure, the clouds are light,
The moonbeams glitter cold and bright;
O'er the wide landscape breathes no sigh;
The sea reflects the star-gemmed sky,
And every beam of heaven's broad brow
Glows brightly on the world below.
But ah! the wing of death is spread;
I hear the midnight murderers' tread;
I hear the Plague that walks at night,
I mark its pestilential blight;
I feel its hot and withering breath,
It is the messenger of death!
And can a scene so pure and fair
Slumber beneath a baneful air?
And can the stealing form of death
Here wither with its blighting breath?
Yes; and the slumberer feels its power
At midnight's dark and silent hour.
He feels the wild-fire through his brain;
He wakes; his frame is racked with pain;
His eye half closed; his lip is dark;
The sword of death hath done his work!
That sallow cheek, that fevered lip,
That eye which burns but cannot sleep,
That black parched tongue, that raging brain,
All mark the monarch's baleful reign!

O! for one pure, one balmy breath,
To cool the sufferer's brow in death ;
O! for one wandering breeze of heaven ;
O that one moment's rest were given!
'Tis past ; and hushed the victim's prayer ;
The spirit *was* — but *is* not there !

RUINS OF PALMYRA.

Palmyra, where art thou, all dreary and lone?
The breath of thy fame, like the night-wind, hath
    flown:
O'er thy temples, thy minarets, towers, and halls
The dark veil of oblivion silently falls.

The sands of the desert sweep by thee in pride,
They curl round thy brow, like the foam of the tide,
And soon, like the mountain stream's wild-rolling
    wave,
Will rush o'er, and wrap thee at once in thy grave.

O, where are the footsteps which once gayly flew
O'er pavements where now weep the foxglove and
    yew?
O, where are the voices which once gayly sung,
While the lofty-browed domes with melody rung?

They are silent; and naught breaks the chaos of
    death;
Not a being now treads o'er the ivy's dull wreath,
Save the raging hyena, whose terrible cry
Echoes loud through the halls and the palaces high.

Thou art fallen, Palmyra! and never to rise,
Thou "queen of the east, thou bright child of the
 skies!"
Thou art lonely; the desert around thee is wide;
Then haste to its arms, nor remember thy pride.

Thou art forgotten, Palmyra! return thee to earth;
And great be thy fall, as was stately thy birth;
With grandeur then bow 'neath the pinion of time,
And sink, not in splendor, but sadly sublime.

THE WIDE WORLD IS DREAR.

O say not the wide world is lonely and dreary!
  O say not that life is a wilderness waste!
There's ever some comfort in store for the weary,
  And there's ever some hope for the sorrowful breast.

There are often sweet dreams which will steal o'er
    the soul,
  Beguiling the mourner to smile through a tear,
That, when waking, the dew-drops of mem'ry may
    fall,
  And blot out, forever, "the wide world is drear."

There is hope for the lost, for the lone one's relief,
  Which will beam o'er his pathway of danger and
    fear ;
There is pleasure's wild throb, and the calm "joy of
    grief,"
  O then say not the wide world is lonely and drear!

There are fears that are anxious, yet sweet to the
    breast.
  Some feelings, which language ne'er told to the ear,
Which return to the heart, and there lingering rest,
  Soft whispering, this world is not lonely and drear.

'Tis true that the dreams of the evening will fade,
  When reason's broad sunbeam shines calmly and
    clear ;
Still fancy, sweet fancy, will smile o'er the shade,
  And say that the world is not lonely and drear.

O then mourn not that life is a wilderness waste !
  That each hope is illusive, each prospect is drear,
But remember that man, undeserving, is blest,
  And rewarded with smiles for the fall of a tear.

FAREWELL TO MISS E. B.

Farewell, and whenever calm solitude's hour
Shall silently spread its broad wings o'er your bower,
O! then gaze on yon planet, yon watch-fire divine,
And believe that my soul is there mingling with
    thine.

When the dark brow of evening is beaming with
    stars,
And yon crest of light clouds is the turban she wears,
When she walks forth in grandeur, the queen of the
    night,
O! then think that my spirit looks on with delight.

O'er the ocean of life our frail vessels are bounding,
And danger and death our dark pathway surrounding;
Destruction's bright meteors are dancing before,
And behind us the winds of adversity roar.

O! then come, let us light friendship's lamp on the
    wave:
If we're lost, it will shed its pure light o'er the grave,
Or 'twill guide to the haven of Heaven at last,
And beam on when the voice of the trumpet hath
    passed.

DEATH.

THE destroyer cometh ; his footstep is light,
He marketh the threshold of sorrow at night ;
He steals like a thief o'er the fond one's repose,
And chills the warm tide from the heart as it flows.

His throne is the tomb, and a pestilent breath
Walks forth on the night-wind, the herald of death ;
His couch is the bier, and the dark weeds of woe
Are the curtains which shroud joy's deadliest foe.

A VIEW OF DEATH.

WHEN bending o'er the brink of life,
 My trembling soul shall stand,
Waiting to pass death's awful flood,
 Great God! at thy command ;

When weeping friends surround my bed,
 To close my sightless eyes ;
When shattered by the weight of years
 This broken body lies ;

When every long-loved scene of life
 Stands ready to depart ;
When the last sigh which shakes this frame,
 Shall rend this bursting heart, —

O Thou great source of joy supreme,
 Whose arm alone can save,
Dispel the darkness that surrounds
 The entrance to the 'grave.

Lay thy supporting, gentle hand
 Beneath my sinking head,
And with a ray of love divine
 Illume my dying-bed.

Leaning on thy dear, faithful breast,
   I would resign my breath,
And in thy loved embraces lose
   The bitterness of death.

ROB ROY'S REPLY TO FRANCIS OSBALDISTONE.

THE heather I trod while breathing on earth,
Must bloom o'er my grave in the land of my birth;
My warm heart would shrink like the fern in the
      frost,
If the tops of my hills to my dim eyes were lost.

ON THE

DEATH OF THE BEAUTIFUL MRS. * * * * *.

I saw her when life's tide was high,
   When youth was hov'ring o'er her brow,
When joy was dancing in her eye,
   And her cheek blushed hope's crimson glow.

I saw her 'mid a fairy throng
   She seemed the gayest of the gay ;
I saw her lightly glide along
   'Neath beauty's smile and pleasure's lay.

I saw her in her bridal robe ;
   The blush of joy was mounting high ;
I marked her bosom's heaving throb,
   I marked her dark and downcast eye.

I saw her when a mother's love
   Asked at her hand a mother's care ;
She looked an angel from above,
   Hovering round a cherub fair.

I saw her not till, cold and pale,
   She slumbered on Death's icy arm ;
The rose had faded on her cheek,
   Her lip had lost its power to charm.

That eye was dim which brightly shone ;
　That brow was cold ; that heart was still ;
The witcheries of that form had flown ;
　The lifeless clay had ceased to feel.

I saw her wedded to the grave ;
　Her bridal robes were weeds of death ;
And o'er her pale, cold brow was hung
　The damp sepulchral icy wreath.

TO MY DEAR MOTHER IN SICKNESS.

Hang not thy harp upon the willow ;
   Mourn not a brighter, happier day :
But touch the chord, and life's wild billow
   Will, shrinking, foam its shame away.

Then strike the chord and raise the strain
   Which brightens that dark clouded brow ;
O ! beam *one* sunshine smile again,
   And I'll forgive thy sadness now.

Though darkness, gloom, and doubt surround thee,
   Thy bark, though frail, shall safely ride ;
The storm and whirlwind may rage round thee,
   But thou wilt all their wrath abide.

Hang not thy harp upon the willow
   Which weeps o'er every passing wave ;
Though life is but a restless pillow,
   There's calm and peace beyond the grave.

KINDAR BURIAL SERVICE.

VERSIFIED.

We commend our brother to thee, O earth!
To thee he returns, from thee was his birth!
Of thee was he formed, he was nourished by thee;
Take the body, O earth! the spirit is free.

O air! he once breathed thee, through thee he
    survived,
And in thee and with thee his pure spirit lived;
That spirit hath fled, and we yield him to thee;
His ashes be spread, like his soul, far and free.

O fire! we commit his dear relics to thee,
Thou emblem of purity, spotless and free:
May his soul, like thy flames, bright and burning
    arise
To its mansion of bliss, in the star-spangled skies.

O water! receive him; without thy kind aid
He had parched 'neath the sunbeams or mourned
    in the shade;
Then take of his body the share which is thine,
For the spirit hath fled from its mouldering shrine.

THE GRAVE.

THERE is a spot so still and dreary,
It is a pillow to the weary ;
It is so solemn and so lone,
That grief forgets to heave a groan.

There life's storms can enter never ;
There 'tis dark and lonely ever ;
The mourner there shall seek repose,
And there the wanderer's journey close.

12

THE ARMY OF ISRAEL AT THE FOOT OF MOUNT SINAI.

THEIR spears glittered bright in the beams of the
    sun ;
Their banners waved far, and their high helmets
    shone ;
And their dark plumes were tossed on the breast of
    the breeze,
But the war-trumpet slumbered the slumber of peace.

He came in his glory, He came in his might,
His chariot the cloud, and his sceptre the light ;
The sound of his coming was heard from afar,
Like the roar of a nation when rushing to war.

'Twas the great God of Israel, riding on high,
Whose footstool is earth, and whose throne is the
    sky ;
He stood in his glory, unseen and alone,
And with letters of fire traced the tablets of stone.

The eagle may soar to the sun in his might,
And the eye of the warrior flash fierce in the fight ;
But say, who may look upon God the Most High ?
O Israel! turn back from his glory, or die.

The sun in its splendor, the fire in its might,
Which devours and withers, and wastes from the
     sight,
Is dim to the glory which beams from his eye;
Then, Israel, turn back — O! return, or ye die.

THE GARDEN OF GETHSEMANE.

Gethsemane! there's holy blood
   Upon thy green and waving brow;
Gethsemane! a God hath stood,
   And o'er thy branches bended low!

There drops of agony have hung
   Mingled with blood upon his brow;
For sin his bosom there was wrung,
   And there it bled for human woe.

There, in the darkest hour of night,
   Alone He watched, alone He prayed;
Didst thou not tremble at the sight?
   A God reviled! a God betrayed!

Gethsemane! so dark a scene
   Ne'er blotted the wide book of time!
Oblivion's veil can never screen
   So dark a deed, so black a crime!

THE TEMPEST GOD.

Hark! 'tis the wheels of his wide-rolling car;
They traverse the heavens and come from afar;
Sublime and majestic the dark cloud he rides,
The wing of the whirlwind he fearlessly strides,
The glance of his eye is the lightning's broad flame,
And the caverns reëcho his terrible name.

In the folds of his pinions the wild whirlwinds sleep;
At his bidding they rush o'er the foam of the deep;
He speaks, and in whispers they murmur to rest,
And calmly they sink on the folds of his breast;
His seat is the mountain-top's loftiest height;
He reigns there in darkness, the king of the night.

TO A DEPARTING FRIEND.

FAREWELL, and may some angel guide,
  Some viewless spirit hover o'er thee;
Who, let or weal or woe betide,
  Will still unchanging move before thee.

A hallowed light shall burn at night,
  When sorrow's wave rolls drearily,
And o'er thy way a cloud by day
  Shall cast its shadow cheerily.

Thy bark of pleasure o'er life's smooth sea
  Shall gallantly glide along;
Prayers and blessings thy breezes shall be,
  And hope be thy parting song.

Go then; I have given the spirits charge
  To watch o'er thee now and forever;
To smooth life's waters, and guide thy barge
  Where tempest shall toss it never.

MARITORNE; OR, THE PIRATE OF MEXICO.

On Barritaria's brow the watch-fires glow,
Their beacons beaming on the Gulf below,
As if to dare some death-devoted hand
To quench in blood the boldly blazing brand ;
Some Orlean herald armed with threat'ning high
To daunt the Pirate Chieftain's haughty eye,
To bid him bend to tame and vulgar law,
And bow to painted things with trembling awe.
Such herald well may come, but woe betide
The self-devoted messenger of pride !
Such herald well may come, but far and near
The name of Maritorne is joined with fear ;
His vessels proudly ride the Gulf at will,
Whilst he is Chief of Barritaria's Isle.
The iron hand of power is raised in vain,
Whilst Maritorne is master of the main.
'Tis his to sacrifice, 'tis his to spare :
He moves in silence, and is everywhere.
His victims must with pompous boldness bleed,
But if he pities, who may tell the deed ?
'Tis done in secret, that no eye may mark
One thought more gentle, or one act less dark.
And he, the Governor of yon fair land,
Whose tongue speaks freedom, but whose guilty hand

Grasps the half-loosened manacles again,
And adds, unseen, fresh links to slavery's chain;
Hated full deeply, dreaded and abhorred,
The Pirate Chief, the haughty island lord.
And cause enough, deep hidden in his breast,
Had *he*, the moody leader of the West,
To hate that fearful man, who stood alone
Feared, dreaded, and detested, though unknown.
That cause was smothered or burst forth to light,
Wreathed in the incense of a patriot's right,
To drive the bold intruder from the shore,
Where war and bloodshed must appear no more;
But deep within his heart the crater glowed
From whence this gilded stream of lava flowed;
'Twas wounded pride, which, writhing inly, bled,
And called for vengeance on the offender's head;
For Maritorne, with bold, unbending brow,
Had scorned his power — that were enough; but lo!
There on the very threshold of his home,
There had the traitor Pirate dared to come,
And thence had borne his own, his only child,
Mate all unfit for Maritorne the wild;
And when the maiden cursed him in her breast,
Those curses came not o'er him, — he was blest:
For but to gaze upon her, and to feel
That she whom he adored was near him still,
Was bliss! was heaven itself! and he whose eye
Bent not to aught of dull mortality,
Shrunk with a tremulous delight whene'er
The voice of Laura rose upon his ear;
That voice had power to quell the fiend within,
Whose touch had turned his very soul to sin.

That fiend was vengeance ; e'en his virtues bowed
Before the altar which to vengeance glowed.
His virtues ! yes ; for even fiends may boast
A shadow of the glory they have lost.
But O ! like them, his crimes were dark and deep,
For vengeance was awake, — can vengeance sleep ;
Yes ; sleep, as tigers sleep, with half-shut eye,
Crouching to spring upon the passer-by,
With parched tongue cleaving to his blackened cell,
Stiff'ning with thirst, and jaws which hunger fell
Hath sharply whetted, quivering to devour
The reckless wretch abandoned to his power.
Yes : thus may vengeance sleep in breast like his,
Where thoughts of wild revenge are thoughts of bliss.
Thus may it sleep, like Ætna's burning breast,
To burst in thunders when 'tis dreaded least ;
For his had been the joyless, thankless part
Of one who warmed a viper at his heart,
And clasped the venomed reptile to his breast
Till wounded by the ingrate he caressed.
Such had been Maritorne's accursed fate,
Ere he became the hardened child of hate.
At first, his breast was torn with anguish wild ;
He cursed himself, then bitterly reviled
The world as hollow-hearted, false, unkind ;
He cursed himself, and doubly cursed mankind ;
And then his heart grew callous, and like steel
Grasped in his hand, had equal power to feel.
'Twas like yon mountain snow-crest, chill though
    bright,
Cold to the touch, but dazzling to the sight,

Till when the hour of darkness gathers, then
The sunbeam fades, the ice grows dim again.
He had a friend, one on whom fancy's eye
Had deeply, rashly stamped fidelity:
Traitor had better seemed — worm —viper — aught —
The vilest, veriest wretch e'er named in thought;
For he was sin's own son, and all that e'er
Angels above may hate or mortals fear.
There was a fascination in his eye
Which those who felt, might seek in vain to fly.
There was a blasting glance of mockery there;
There was a calm, contemptuous, biting sneer
Forever on his lip, which made men fear,
And, fearing, shun him, as a bird will shun
A gilded bait, though glittering in the sun;
But still the mask of friendship he could wear;
The smile, the warm professions all were there;
Let him who trusts to these alone, beware!
A lurking devil may be crouching there.
Shame on mankind that they will stoop to use
Wiles which the imps of darkness would refuse.
Henceforth let friendship drop her robes of light,
And following desolation's blasting flight

     .   .   .   .

    .   .   .   .   .

There paced the Pirate Chief with giant stride,
Deep chorus keeping to the Mexic tide;
His sable plumes were hovering o'er his brow,
As if to hide the depth of thought below.
He paused — 'twas but the dashing of the spray;
Again! 'twas but the night-watch on his way.

He only muttered, gnashed his teeth, and smiled;
Fit mirth were that, so ghastly and so wild,
To grace a Pirate Chieftain's scornful lip;
'Twas like St. Helmo's night-fire o'er the deep.
The beacon blaze is burning on the shore,
But burns it not more dimly than before?
Perchance the drowsy sentinel is sleeping,
His weary vigils negligently keeping.
So thought the Chief, but still his wary eye
Was fixed intently between earth and sky,
As if its quick, keen glance would light the flame,
And blast the sleeper with remorse and shame.
He starts; suspicion flashes on his brain --
He grasps his dagger — by St. Mark — again!
His bugle brightly glittered on his breast;
His lip the gilded bauble gently pressed;
One breath, one sigh, and rock and hill and sea
Will echo back the warlike minstrelsy.
The figure which had slowly passed between
Himself and yonder blaze, sank where 'twas seen,
As though the earth had gaped with sudden yawn,
And drank both fire and form in silence down;
The beacon was extinguished, rock and tree
And beetling cliff, and wildly foaming sea,
Were hid in darkness, for the deep red light
Which faintly sketched them on the brow of night,
Was dim as was the moon's pale tremulous glow,
For tempest-clouds were rallying round her brow;

The sound of a footstep is on the shore,
It dies away in the surge's roar;
It is heard again as the angry spray
Rolls back and foams its shame away;
And shrill and clear was the call of alarm, —
'Twas like the breaking of spell or charm;
It screamed o'er the dark wave, it rose to the hill,
And the answering echoes reëchoed it still.
A rushing sound as of coming waves,
A glittering band as if burst from their graves,
Are the answers which wake at the bidding clear
Of him, the Lord of the Isle of Fear.
But scarce had the summons in silence died,
When the foot which had waked the tumult wide,
Was pressing the sand where it yielding gave
To the lightest tread as 'twas washed by the wave;
By the side of the Pirate, with outstretched hand,
The bold intruder looked round on the band;
But none saw the face of that being save he;
In wonder he gazed; in his eye you might see
Surprise, and shame, and a fiend-like gleam,
Which whispered of more than fear might dream;
" And is it for this — for a woman like thee?"
He angrily muttered and turned to the sea —
" And is it for this I have sounded the call
Whose notes may never unanswered fall;
Whose lowest tone is the knell of more
Than can crowd at once upon Hell's broad shore?
And is it for this I must idly stand
To trace the wave with my sword on the strand?

Speak! tell me, or now, by the blood on its blade,
I will give to that pale cheek a deadlier shade."
"The beacon! the beacon!" — she turned to the spot,
And pointed the Chief where the light was not.
The murmur ran through the waiting crowd;
It was loud at first, but it grew more loud,
Till "the *Beacon!* the *Beacon!*" rang on to the sky,
But its light was extinguished, no blaze met the eye.
"Thus much for the moment; thy honor is clear;
If it suffers, then look for thy recompense here:"
And she threw back her mantle and gave to the
   light
Which glared from the torches all flamingly bright,
A form which e'en Maritorne marked not unmoved,
But 'twas one which he did not, nor ever had loved.
"There are spies who are waiting in ambush for thee,
I marked out the cavern; 'twas near to the sea;
They are few, they are bold, they are guided by one
Who has sworn ere the dawn of another day's sun
To lead thee in triumph, unwounded, unharmed,
To yonder proud city all chained and unarmed;
This swears he by all that is sacred to do,
I heard it and hastened thus breathless to you.
For pardon I sue not; O punish my crime!
Here, here is my bosom, and now is the time!
The last moment beheld me imploring for breath,
Now 'tis not worth asking, I sue but for death."
The ocean was roaring too loudly to hear
The words she was speaking, the Chief bent his ear;
His dark plume was resting half fearfully there,
Upon the white brow of the beautiful Clare,

As a being all guilty and trembling would rest
Self-accused, self-condemned, in the land of the blest.
And he, its wild wearer, how heard he the tale?
His eye flashed the darker, his lip grew more pale;
But when it was finished and Clara knelt down,
Where, where was his anger, and where was his
          frown?
On her forehead he printed a passionate kiss.
" O Clara, forgive me! remember not this,
But forget not that thou, and thou only, shalt know
The cause of my madness, my guilt, and my woe.
If I fall, thou wilt read it in letters of blood
'Neath the stone, near the rock, where the beacon-
          light glowed;
If I live," — and he hastily bowed himself, — " then
The Fiend and the pirate were masters again."

       .   .   .

A light is on the waters, and the dip
Of distant oars is heard from steep to steep:
The hum of voices float upon the air,
Soft, yet distinct, though distant, full and clear.
Come they to Barritaria's Isle as midnight foes?
'Tis well! the world but roughly with them goes.
Come they to Barritaria's Isle to join
Their traitor arms, proud Maritorne, with thine?
O, better had they never left yon shore,
To which they may return again no more;
Fools! think they he is bleeding in a strife
Where every drop writes guilt upon his life
For gold, for fame, for power, for aught on earth

Which vulgar minds might think were richly worth
A life of bloodshed and dishonor? No!
They read not right who read yon pirate so;
The plash of troubled waters, and the sound
Of moving vessels grating o'er the ground,
The quick low hum of voices, the faint gush
Of light waves gurgling as with sudden rush
They feebly kissed the bark, then sunk away,
As half-repenting them such welcome gay,
Were caught, perchance, by some lone fisher's ear,
Who plied his line or net at midnight here;
Perhaps he started from his drowsy mood,
And tossed his bait still further down the flood;
But be that as it may, 'twas heard no more,
And list'ning silence hovered o'er the shore.
And yonder fire the battle sign is beaming,
Far o'er the dusky waters redly streaming.
The shadow of the Pirate-ship lies there,
Its banners feebly dancing in the air;
Its broad sails veering idly to and fro,
Now glitt'ring 'neath the full moon's silver glow,
Now black'ning in the shade of night's dull frown;
'Twas like its Chief, in silence and alone,
Gazing upon the shadow which it cast
O'er every rippling wave which gently passed.
And such had been his joyless, gloomy lot,
Forgetting all mankind, by all forgot,
Save that accursed one whose blasting eye
Was glaring on him, — 'twas in vain to fly
While vengeance whispered curses in his ear,
And thought, the demon thought, received them there.

But it had ever been his lot to throw
O'er those who passed him, shades of gloom and woe ;
His love for Laura had been deeply cursed ;
Hatred's black phial o'er his brow had burst ;
He felt himself detested, and he knew
That she whom he adored, abhorred him too.
But O, the hapless, the ill-fated one,
She who could love him for himself alone,
Love him with all the crimes upon his head,
Love when the crowd with detestation fled, —
A deep dark shade, a wild, a with'ring blast
Fell o'er her destiny ; the die was cast ;
She was a wretched one, a sweet flower faded,
Whose   wand'ring   tendrils   round   the   night-shade
        braided,
Clung to its baleful breast, — hung drooping there,
Self-sacrificed, it drank the poisoned air
And with'ring   .   .   .   .
    1825.   [*Unfinished.*]

AMERICA.

And this was once the realm of Nature, where
Wild as the wind, though exquisitely fair,
She breathed the mountain breeze, or bowed to kiss
The dimpling waters with unbounded bliss.
Here in this Paradise of earth, where first
Wild mountain Liberty began to burst,
Once Nature's temple rose in simple grace,
The hill her throne, the world her dwelling-place.
And where are now her lakes, so still and lone,
Her thousand streams with bending shrubs o'ergrown?
Where her dark cat'racts tumbling from on high,
With rainbow arch aspiring to the sky?
Her tow'ring pines with fadeless wreaths entwined,
Her waving alders streaming to the wind?
Nor these alone, — her own, — her fav'rite child,
All fire, all feeling; man untaught and wild;
Where can the lost, lone son of Nature stray?
For art's high car is rolling on its way;
A wand'rer of the world, he flies to drown
The thoughts of days gone by and pleasures flown
In the deep draught, whose dregs are death and woe,
With slavery's iron chain concealed below.
Once through the tangled wood, with noiseless tread
And throbbing heart, the lurking warrior sped,
Aimed his sure weapon, won the prize, and turned,
While his high heart with wild ambition burned,

13

With song and war-whoop to his native tree,
There on its bark to carve the victory.
His all of learning did that act comprise,
But still in *nature's* volume doubly wise.

The wayward stream which once, with idle bound,
Whirled on resistless in its foaming round,
Now curbed by art flows on, a wat'ry chain
Linking the snow-capped mountains to the main.
Where once the alder in luxuriance grew,
Or the tall pine its towering branches threw
Abroad to heaven, with dark and haughty brow,
There mark the realms of plenty smiling now ;
There the full sheaf of Ceres richly glows,
And Plenty's fountain blesses as it flows ;
And man, a brute when left to wander wild,
A reckless creature, Nature's lawless child,
What boundless streams of knowledge rolling now
From the full hand of art around him flow !
Improvement strides the surge, while from afar
Learning rolls onward in her silver car ;
Freedom unfurls her banner o'er his head,
While peace sleeps sweetly on her native bed.

The Muse arises from the wild-wood glen,
And chants her sweet and hallowed song again,
As in those halcyon days, which bards have sung,
When hope was blushing, and when life was young.
Thus shall she rise, and thus her sons shall rear
Her sacred temple *here*, and only *here*,

While Percival, her loved and chosen priest,
Forever blessing, though himself unblest,
Shall fan the fire that blazes at her shrine,
And charm the ear with numbers half divine.

LINES ADDRESSED TO A COUSIN.

She gave me a flow'ret, — and O ! it was sweet !
  'Twas a pea in full bloom, with its dark crimson
     leaf,
And I said in my heart, this shall be thy retreat !
  'Tis one "sacred to Friendship" — a stranger to
     grief.

In my bosom I placed it, — 'tis withered and gone !
  All its freshness, its beauty, its fragrance had fled !
And in sorrow I sighed, — Am I *thus* left alone ?
  Is the gift which I cherished quite faded and dead ?

It has withered ! but *she* who presented it blooms,
  Still fresh and unfading, in memory *here !*
And through life shall *here* flourish, 'mid danger and
     glooms,
  As sweet as the flower, though more lasting and
     fair !

ON SEEING A YOUNG LADY AT HER DEVO-TIONS.

SHE knelt, and her dark blue eye was raised, —
A sacred fire in its bright beam blazed,
And it spread o'er her cold pale cheek a light
So pure and so sacred, so clear and so bright,
That Parian marble, though glittering fair
'Neath the moon's pale beam or the sun's broad
     glare,
Were far less sweet, though more dazzlingly bright,
Than that cold cheek arrayed in its halo of light.
O ! I love not the dark rosy hue of the sky
When the bright blush of morn mantles deeply and
     high,
But my fond soul adores the pure author of light,
The more when she looks on the broad brow of
     night ;
On myriads of stars glitt'ring far through the sky,
Like the bright eyes of saints looking down from on
     high
From their garden of Paradise, blooming in heaven,
On the scene sleeping sweet 'neath the calm smile of
     even.

I love not the cheek which speaks slumber unbroken ;
That heart hath ne'er sighed o'er hope's fast fading
     token ;

That bosom ne'er throbbed with half fearful delight
When it thought on its home in the regions of light,
Or trembled and wept as with fancy's dear eye
It gazed on the beautiful gates of the sky,
And the angels which watch at their portals of light
All peaceful, all sacred, all pure, and all bright;
But I love that pale cheek as it bends in devotion,
Like a star sinking down on the breast of the ocean.

1825.

TO A YOUNG LADY,

WHOSE MOTHER WAS INSANE FROM HER BIRTH.

AND thou hast never, never known
   A mother's love, a mother's care!
Hast wept, and sighed, and smiled alone,
   Unblest by e'en a mother's prayer.

O, if sad sorrow's blighting hand
   Hath e'er an arrow, it is this:
To feel that frenzy's burning brand
   Hath wiped away a mother's kiss;

To mark the gulf, the starless wave,
   Which rolls between thee and her love;
To feel that better were a grave,
   A grave beneath, a home above,

Than thus that she should linger on,
   In dreamless, sunless solitude,
Like some bright ruined shrine, where one
   All loveliness and truth hath stood.

And he, her love, her life, her light,
   How burst the storm o'er him!
O, darker than Egyptian night, —
   'Twas one wild troubled dream!

To gaze upon that eye, whose beam
    Was love, and life, and light,
To mark its wild and wandering gleam
    Which dazzles but to blight;

To turn in anguish and despair
    From those wild notes of sadness,
And feel that there was darkness there,
    The midnight mist of madness;

To start beneath the thrilling swell
    Of notes still sweet, though wasted,
To mark the idol loved too well,
    In all its beauty blasted;

O! it were better far to kneel,
    In darkly brooding anguish,
Upon the graves of those we love,
    Than *thus* to see them languish.

THE FEAR OF MADNESS.

WRITTEN WHILE CONFINED TO HER BED, DURING HER LAST ILLNESS.

THERE is a something which I dread,
    It is a dark, a fearful thing ;
It steals along with withering tread,
    Or sweeps on wild destruction's wing.

That thought comes o'er me in the hour
    Of grief, of sickness, or of sadness ;
'Tis not the dread of death — 'tis more,
    It is the dread of madness.

O ! may these throbbing pulses pause,
    Forgetful of their feverish course ;
May this hot brain, which, burning, glows
    With all its fiery whirlpool's force,

Be cold, and motionless, and still,
    A tenant of its lowly bed,
But let not dark delirium steal —

  .   .   .   .

                            [Unfinished.]

1825.

MY LAST FAREWELL TO MY HARP.

AND must we part? yes, part forever?
I'll waken thee again — no, never;
Silence shall chain thee cold and drear,
And thou shalt calmly slumber here.
Unhallowed was the eye that gazed
Upon the lamp which brightly blazed,
The lamp which never can expire,
The undying, wild, poetic fire.
And O! unhallowed was the tongue
Which boldly and uncouthly sung;
I blessed the hour when o'er my soul
Thy magic numbers gently stole,
And o'er it threw those heavenly strains,
Which since have bound my heart in chains;
Those wild, those witching numbers still
Will o'er my widowed bosom steal.
I blessed that hour, but O! my heart,
Thou and thy lyre must part; yes, part;
And this shall be my last farewell,
This my sad bosom's latest knell.
And here, my harp, we part forever;
I'll waken thee again, O! never;
Silence shall chain thee cold and drear,
And thou shalt calmly slumber here.

PROSE COMPOSITION.

———◆———

COLUMBUS.

WHAT must have been the feelings of Christopher Columbus, when, for the first time, he knelt and clasped his hands, in gratitude, upon the shores of his newly discovered world? Year after year has rolled away; war, famine, and fire have alternately swept the face of that country; the hand of tyranny hath oppressed it; the footstep of the slave hath wearily trodden it; the blood of the slaughtered hath dyed it; the tears of the wretched have bedewed it; still, even at this remote period, every feeling bosom will delight to dwell upon this brilliant era in the life of the persevering adventurer. At that moment, his name was stamped upon the records of history forever; at that moment, doubt, fear, and anxiety fled, for his foot had pressed upon the threshold of the promised land.

The bosom of Columbus hath long since ceased to beat; its hopes, its fears, its projects, sleep, with him, the long and dreamless slumber of the grave; but while there remains one generous pulsation in the human breast, his name and his memory will be held sacred.

When the cold dews of uncertainty stood upon his brow; when he beheld nothing but the wide heavens above, the boundless waters beneath and around him; himself and his companions in that little bark, the only beings upon the endless world of sky and ocean; when he looked back, and thought upon his native land; when he looked forward, and in vain traversed the liquid desert for some spot upon which to fix the aching eye of anxiety, — O! say, amidst all these dangers, these uncertainties, whence came that high, unbending hope, which still soared onward to the world before him? whence that undying patience, that more than mortal courage, which forbade his cheek to blanch amid the storm, or his heart to recoil in the dark and silent hour of midnight? It was from God — it was of God — His Spirit overshadowed the adventurer! By day, an unseen cloud directed him; by night, a brilliant, but invisible column moved before him, gleaming athwart the boundless waste of waters. The winds watched over him, and the waves upheld him, for God was with him; the whirlwind passed over his little bark, and left it still riding onward, in safety, towards its unknown harbor, for the eye of Him who pierces the deep was fixed upon it.

Columbus had hoped, feared, and had been disappointed; he had suffered long and patiently; he had strained every faculty, every nerve; he had pledged his very happiness upon the discovery of an unknown land; and what must have been the feelings of his soul, when, at length bending over that very land, his grateful bosom offered its tribute of praise and thanksgiving to the Being who had guarded and guided him through death and danger? He beheld the bitter smile of scorn and derision fade before the reality of that vision which had been ridiculed and mocked at; he thought upon the thousand obstacles which he had surmounted; he thought upon those who had regarded him as a self-devoted enthusiast, a visionary madman; and his full heart throbbed in gratitude to Him whose Spirit had inspired him, whose voice had sent him forth, and whose arm had protected him.

1824.

ALPHONSO IN SEARCH OF LEARNING.

AN ALLEGORY.

EARLY one morning Alphonso set out in search of Learning. He travelled over barren heaths and over rocks, and was often obliged to ford rivers which seemed almost impassable; at last, completely exhausted, and at a loss what road to take, he sat down desponding by the side of a rapid river. Soon a passenger approached, with whom Alphonso entered into conversation, and at length asked him where he was going. "I am," replied the stranger, "seeking Fame; and already by her trump has my name been sounded in her courts. She has promised to *immortalize* my name; follow me, and you shall richly reap the reward of your labor." "I also," answered Alphonso, "have a road to pursue, which leads to Fame; but it is through Learning that I must reach her courts, and then shall I enjoy the fruits of my toil, in proportion to the hardships with which I have acquired it. Can you tell me where she can be found?"

"You see," replied the stranger, "yonder hills which rise one upon the other, as far as the eye extends; far, far beyond *them*, whose every precipice you have to climb, Learning resides. Her temple is pleasant, but few there are who gain it; many, indeed, have gone beyond these foremost hills, but stumbling, they have been dashed to pieces on the rocks; but still they have had the reputation of having reached her temple, and their names are recorded in the roll of Fame." Thus saying, the stranger proceeded on his journey, and left Alphonso in doubt whether to pursue the dangerous road of which the stranger had warned him, or to follow him to more easily acquired fame.

At last Wisdom came to his assistance, and he resolved not to give up his search after Learning. He proceeded therefore, and had reached the foot of the hill, when he was met by another person, who inquired whither he was going. "I am in pursuit of Learning," replied Alphonso. "What! do you intend climbing yonder rugged and tiresome hill?" "I do," answered Alphonso.

"Indolence is my companion," said the stranger: "I found her in yonder valley. I toiled not for her, and without toil I enjoy ease; on the other hand, Learning cannot be obtained without labor; go with me, and you shall enjoy life." Alphonso, partly fatigued with his long walk, and partly discouraged by the rugged appearance of the hill, consented. After walking on some time in a beautiful valley, Alphonso began to discover that his new companion was flat and insipid, that he had exhausted all his little fund of knowledge in the beginning of their journey, and that he now scarcely said anything. Thus continuing dissatisfied, not with the path, but with the companion he had, they entered a beautiful meadow, in which there was an arbor, called the arbor of Indolence, and there they lay down to rest; but before Alphonso slept, a warning voice sounded in his ear, "Awake, for destruction is at hand." He heeded it not, and with his senses slept his conscience.

When they arose to pursue their journey, a tempest gathered ; thick clouds were in the heavens ; all was black. Night's sable mantle was thrown over the horizon, and only now and then a flash of lightning, attended with a dreadful thunderbolt, showed them both the dead waters of oblivion ; near them was the path which slides the unhappy deluded mortal down to its deep and noisome bed.

Alphonso's conductor, who had before appeared certain of being on safe ground, trembled and turned pale when he found himself in the fatal path. Alphonso was on the brink ! He receded ; his flesh grew cold, his eyeballs glared, and his hair stood on end. Presently he heard a low plashing of the dead waters of oblivion ; they closed with a sullen roar over the unhappy sufferer, and all was silent. "This is the end of the careless votary of Indolence," thought Alphonso, as he turned from the dead waters of the lake. "Let this be a lesson to me !"

He stood in deep perplexity some time, not daring to turn back, and he knew it would be certain death to proceed ; but suddenly the clouds dispersed, the air was calm, and all was silent ; he blessed the returning light, and with new vigor passed on his way in search of Learning. He was overjoyed when he found himself out of the fatal vale of Indolence.

Again he viewed those hills which so discouraged him when they met his eye before ; but now they appeared to him with a far different aspect, as he traced over them the path to Learning's happy temple.

He began his journey anew, and as he proceeded, the ascent was easier. When he reached the top of the hill, a few faint rays of the bright sun of Learning warmed his heart, and though faint, it was sufficient to kindle the slumbering fire of hope in his bosom. After he had reached the valley below, he saw a person crossing on the opposite side with a light step and an open, ingenuous countenance.

Alphonso stopped him, and inquired why he did not ascend the hill before him. "Because," said the stranger, " I seek Truth, and she dwells in the simple vale of Innocence; at her court there is no pomp, but there is peace; she discloses her name to all; some revile her, others say she is of no use to the world, that they are always as victorious without her assistance as with it. Her followers scarce ever suffer from the imputations of the vile, when they hold fast upon her garments. I can possess Truth and Innocence without Learning." Here the travellers parted — Alphonso to ascend the hill, the stranger to the vale of Innocence.

Without a companion in his solitary journey, with no one to assist him on his way, no one to raise him if he stumbled, Alphonso pursued his toilsome course. At length, casting his eyes to the top of the hill, he perceived standing on its summit a figure stretching out one hand to assist him, the other rested on an anchor, and a bright beam played around her brow. Alphonso hastened to ascend the hill; and when he approached, he clasped the outstretched hand of Hope, for that was the name of the fair form, and imprinted it with kisses. Hope smiled affectionately upon him, and with these encouraging

14

words addressed him: "Alphonso! I came to conduct you to the temple of Learning; you have overcome, alone, the greatest obstacles; you shall now have a conductor."

As they came to frightful precipices, where unfortunate mortals had been dashed headlong, for daring to approach too near the edge, Hope would catch his hand and conduct him to safer ground. At last, through many difficulties, hazards, and reproaches, Alphonso came in sight of the temple of Learning. The sun was just sinking, and it illumed the edges of the fleecy floating clouds with a golden hue. Its last beam played upon the glittering spire of the temple; Alphonso could scarce believe his eyes. They reached the threshold. After so many toils, so many dangers, he had now acquired the object of his hopes.

They stood a moment, when the door was opened by a grave-looking old man, who heartily welcomed them to the temple. As they entered, all was light: it burst upon his sight like some enchanted scene, where none but ethereal beings dwell. Irresistibly he cast his eyes up to the nave of the spacious hall, and beheld Learning seated upon a throne of gold. A bright sun emitted its cheering rays above his head. In one hand she held a globe, in the other a pen. Books were piled up in great order here, and in another place they were strewn in wild profusion. Ten of her favorite disciples were ranged on either hand; the swift-winged Genius with his beloved companion, Fancy, were seated at her right hand, and often did Genius cast an approving smile at the mistress of his heart and actions: she who had tamed the wild spirit of his temper, and taught it to follow in gentler, softer, and sweeter murmurs.

Hope now conducted Alphonso to the throne of Learning. She smiled as he humbly kneeled at her footstool, and taking a laurel from the hand of the delighted and willing Genius, she crowned the brow of the elated Alphonso. Fancy for a moment deserted the side of Genius and hovered over his laurel-crowned brow; then, clapping her wings in delight, she again resumed her former station. Learning stretched forth her hand to him; "Arise," said she, "you are destined by fate to fill this long vacant seat." Alphonso kissed the outstretched hand, and gratefully took his seat at the side of *Learning.*

1819.

SENSIBILITY.

In this delicate emotion of the human mind there is a mixture of danger and delight ; it may be indulged moderately, with pleasure to its possessor, but uncontrolled, it brings in its train a succession of ideal miseries, and sensations of acute pain or exquisite delight.

It often causes the heart to shrink with sensitive horror from difficulties in the path of life, slightly noticed, or scarcely perceptible to the mind well governed by reason, or fortified by principle. Lively sensibility may be considered as the key-stone of the heart ; it often unguardedly unlocks the treasures confided to its care, and pouring forth the full tide of feeling, the warmest impulses of the soul are wasted upon trifles or squandered on objects insignificant to the eye of reason, and frequently exposes the feeling heart to contempt and ridicule.

Deep and delicate sensibility, that feeling of the soul which shrinks from observation and pours itself forth in secret calm retirement, must certainly, by its dignity and sacred character, cause feelings of reverence for its possessor. Jesus wept over the grave of his departed friend ; his sensibility was aroused, and He shed tears of sorrow over the dark wreck of a once noble fabric in the mouldering remnants of mortality before him. His prophetic soul gazed upon wide scenes of future desolation. He felt for the miseries of mankind ; He pitied their folly and wept over the final destruction of the human frame, undermined by sin and borne down by death.

THE HOLY WRITINGS.

THROUGH the whole of this sacred volume may be traced the finger of a God! It is overshadowed by his arm, and his spirit walks forth in the sublimity of his commandments. What are the mad revilings of the scoffer? They are like burning coals which fall back upon the head of him who hurled them, leaving the object of his rage uninjured. What are the most philosophic works of mankind when placed in comparison with it? They sink into nothing. What are the brilliant shafts of human wit when directed against it? They are as the gilded wing of the butterfly, fluttering feebly against the nervous, the resistless pinion of an eagle. What are all the immense magazines of learning beside it, but a boundless heap of chaff? Yes; the vast edifices of human knowledge reared by the restless hand of ingenuity, and bedecked with all the gaudy trappings of eloquence, crumble into dust and fall prostrate in its presence, as did the heathen idol before the ark of the living God!

Do we ask eloquence? Where can it be found more pure than from the mouth of Him whose voice of mercy is a murmur, and whose anger speaks in wrathful thunders? Do we ask sublimity? The eagle in its flight toward heaven is less sublime than the hallowed words of its Maker. Do we ask simplicity? What is more touchingly so than the language of the sacred volume? Do we ask sweetness or tenderness? The breath of summer is less sweet than the Almighty's offered mercies. The fabled bird which sheds her blood for the nourishment of her innocent offspring, is cruel in comparison with Him, who bled, who died, for those who cursed and tortured Him. Do we ask grandeur, wildness, or strength ? Look there ! there upon the law of Him whose very self is grandeur, whose glance is lightning, and whose arm is strength.

The hand of the impious and the envious may hurl the dust of derision upon this sacred volume : still it will shine on, brighter and brighter, while time shall be !

CHARITY.

THE sacred volume exhorts us to Charity. How carefully, then, should we cherish this kindly feeling, this spark from the fountain of life, that it may beam forth undimmed, and, with its pure and friendly light, cast a ray over our many imperfections, in that day when all will stand in need of mercy and forbearance!

It is not the bare distribution of alms to the needy and suffering beggar, it is not the pompous offerings of opulence to the shrinking child of poverty, which constitutes true charity; no, it is to be understood in a far wider sense; it is forbearing to join with the multitude, when trampling upon a fallen fellow-creature. It is the voice of Charity which pleads for the wretched and the penitent, which raises the prostrate, and whispers forgiveness for the past, and hope for the future. It is her hand which pours the balm of consolation into the lacerated bosom of the returning wanderer, who dares not look back upon the past, and whose heart shrinks as it meets the cold and averted glances of those who in the hour of its pride had bowed before it.

We are all liable to err. Let us make the situation of the suffering penitent our own. Where are the friends we had fondly fancied ours? fled, as from the breath of pestilence, and we are desolate; left with the arrow of adversity rankling in our bosoms, like the stricken deer by the selfish herd, to perish in solitude and wretchedness.

There is no heart so hardened and depraved, that it will not, when the soft voice of Charity whispers peace and forgiveness, yield like wax beneath the hand which stamps it. Then is the moment to impress upon it the sacred precepts of virtue, and to place the bright rewards of penitence before it. "Let us, then, do as we would that others should do unto us;" have mercy upon the fallen, and stretch forth the hand of Charity to the suffering and the penitent.

REMARKS ON THE IMMORALITY OF THE STAGE.

WHY is it that the ear of modesty must be shocked by the indelicacy and immorality which obstinately clings to the stage, that vehicle of good or evil, that splendid engine whose movements may shed a halo of brilliancy around it, or leave behind the blackened traces of its desolating progress?

Can the eye of innocence gaze even upon the mimic characters of vice, or the ear of delicacy become familiarized to the rude and boisterous, or the more dangerously subtle insinuations of depravity, without quitting the fascinating scene less fastidious in its feelings, less sensible to the bold intrusions of barefaced wickedness? No: though the change be slow and almost imperceptible, still it will not be the less certain; the fatal poison will creep to the very vitals of virtue, and stamp deep stains upon the spotless tablet of innocence.

Must, then, all that is bright and pure be shut out from those scenes of fascination, and delight? Must that very purity which should be cherished and guarded as a sacred deposit, be converted into a chain wherewith to shackle the amusements of its possessor? Would not the frequent indulgence of this amusement be holding forth a strong temptation to those who are but partially fortified in the principles of rectitude to overleap the crumbling ill-formed barrier, and plunge at once into the boundless ocean of vice and immorality?

O why will not authors, those helmsmen in the mighty vessel of improvement, dash the countless stains from the charts which they are holding to our eyes, and transform their blackened pages to pure, spotless records of truth and virtue? Then we should no longer mark the blush of offended modesty mantling the cheek of sensibility, or the frown of disapprobation clouding the pure brow of refinement and morality. The stage would then become the guardian and the friend, instead of the fell destroyer of all that is pure and virtuous in the human breast.

CONTEMPLATION OF THE HEAVENS.

To count the glittering millions of the sky, to marshal them in bright array before us, to mark the brilliant traces of a Creator's presence, the foot-prints of the Deity, is a hallowed and sublime employment of the soul ; for being insensibly led onward from gazing upon the portals of heaven, the wonderful threshold of God's wide pavilion, it dares to lift itself in pure and unearthly communion with the Holy Spirit that inhabits there, and to bow in adoration and praise before the great I AM.

To a feeling mind, the heavens unroll a vast volume, filled with subjects of wonder, love, and praise, — wonder, at the inconceivable majesty and goodness of the great Creator of so vast, so splendid a system ; love, for his condescension in deigning to bend his attention to so insignificant a creature as man, even in the meridian of his earthly glory ; and praise for his unchangeable benevolence, infinite wisdom, and perfection. What hand but that of a God could have formed the wide solar system above us ? what voice but that of Him who created them, could bid the starry millions move on for thousands of ages in one unbroken and unceasing march ? The lights of heaven are bright and beautiful, still they are but feeble beams from the everlasting fountain of splendor, or wandering sparks of heaven's dazzling glory. Well indeed might Zoroaster, in the enthusiasm of his heart, worship the fires of heaven as parts of that ineffable and never-dying spirit which animates and lives in all, through all eternity.

In the dark ages of superstition and bigotry, was it strange that he should turn in disgust from the sacrifices of blood, from horrid images, the disgraceful productions of weak bewildered minds, to a fount of pure, unchanging, living light; to the brilliant fires above him, holding their unbroken paths through heaven, pointing to God's throne, and whispering to the heart of something still more bright, more beautiful and holy?

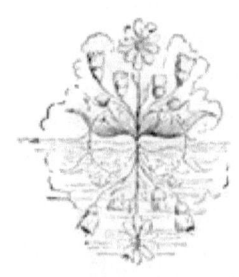

THE ORIGIN OF CHIVALRY.

When society first began to form itself, rank and authority became necessary to subdue the wild and impetuous passions which raged unbridled in the savage bosom of man. Oppression and vassalage first appeared in the form of feudal government; each family looked up to its head, as each kingdom does now to its sovereign; his will was absolute, and his power unbounded in his castle and dominions.

In this way the rights of man were partially secured; the vassal was bound to serve and succor his lord in the hour of danger, as it was that lord's only duty to support and protect his serf. But in those rude and barbarous ages, where was weak and helpless woman to find a shelter from the wild and lawless multitude? and what tribunal was there to which she could appeal if injured? When man was contending with man for superiority, or right, where could she fly for redress? could the feeble voice of woman be heard amid the uproar? No! but it arose, though in murmurs, to the ear of her Maker, and that very evil which menaced her destruction, proved her blessing.

In the dark ages of the world, woman held not that rank in society which a more enlightened age has allotted her; she was deemed merely the slave of man's tyrannical will, the tool of his pleasure, — too weak to defend herself, and too insignificant to claim the pro-

tection of the lords of the creation. As the sun of Religion arose upon the world, the dark clouds of conten-
tion arose with its light ; arms were the arguments
which were unanimously chosen to decide every con-
troversy ; the sword was the test of merit ; and the
hand which wielded it with the greatest dexterity was
chosen to direct the community.

The youthful soldier, ardent and enthusiastic, was ever
in search of some object on which to display his valor ;
the fair sex at length caught and fixed his attention ;
tournaments and feats of arms were instituted to display his devotion to the cause of beauty and virtue in distress, and love and religion were blended ; love became
wildly romantic, religion was enthusiastically venerated ;
the name of woman was held sacred as that of religion ;
and both, as dear to the heart of every knight-errant
as that of the idol, Honor ! they were blended with
each other ; the passions held the reins, and religion,
though contemplated with enthusiasm, was too often
made to bow before the shrine of love and romance.

BIOGRAPHY

OF

LUCRETIA MARIA DAVIDSON.*

———•———

LUCRETIA MARIA DAVIDSON was born at Plattsburg, in the State of New York, on the 27th of September, 1808. Her father, Dr. Oliver Davidson, is a lover of science, and a man of intellectual tastes. Her mother, Margaret Davidson (born Miller), is of a most respectable family, and received the best education her times afforded, at the school of the celebrated Scottish lady, Isabella Graham, an institution in the city of New York, that had no rival in its day, and which derived advantages from the distinguished individual that presided over it that can scarcely be counterbalanced by the multiplied masters and multiform studies of the present day. The family of Miss Davidson lived in seclusion. Their pleasures and excitements were intellectual. Her mother has suffered year after year from ill health and debility; and being a person of imaginative character, and most ardent and susceptible feelings, employed on domestic incidents, and concentrated in maternal tenderness, she naturally loved and cherished her daughter's marvelous gifts, and added to the intensity of the fire with which her genius and her affections, mingling in one holy flame, burned till they consumed their mortal investments. We should not

* Written by Miss Sedgwick, in the year 18 .

have ventured to say thus much of the mother, who still survives to weep and to rejoice over her dead child more than many parents over their living ones, were it not to prove that Lucretia Davidson's character was not miraculous, but that this flower of paradise was nurtured and trained by natural means and influences.

The physical delicacy of this fragile creature was apparent in infancy. When eighteen months old, she had a typhus fever, which threatened her life ; but nature put forth its mysterious energy, and she became stronger and healthier than before her illness. No records were made of her early childhood, save that she was by turns very gay and very thoughtful, exhibiting thus early these common manifestations of extreme sensibility. Her first literary acquisition indicated her after course. She learned her letters at once. At the age of four she was sent to the Plattsburg Academy, where she learned to read and to form letters in sand, after the Lancasterian method. As soon as she could read, her books drew her away from the plays of childhood, and she was constantly found absorbed in the little volumes that her father lavished upon her. Her mother, on some occasion, in haste to write a letter, looked in vain for a sheet of paper. A whole quire had strangely disappeared from the table on which the writing implements usually lay ; she expressed a natural vexation. Her little girl came forward, confused, and said, " Mamma, I have used it." Her mother, knowing she had never been taught to write, was amazed, and asked what possible use she could have for it. Lucretia burst into tears, and replied that " she did not like to tell." Her mother respected the childish mystery, and made no farther inquiries. The paper continued to vanish, and the child was often observed with pen and ink, still sedulously shunning observation. At last her mother, on seeing her make a blank book, asked what she was going to do with it. Lucretia blushed, and left the room without replying. This sharpened her mother's curiosity; she watched the child narrowly, and saw that she made quantities of these little books, and that she was disturbed by observation; and if one of the family requested to see them, she would burst into tears, and run away to hide her secret treasure.

The mystery remained unexplained till she was six years old, when her mother, in exploring a closet rarely opened, found, behind piles of linen, a parcel of papers which proved to be Lucretia's manuscript books. At first the hieroglyphics seemed to baffle investigation. On one side of the leaf was an artfully sketched picture; on the other, Roman letters, some placed upright, others horizontally, obliquely, or backwards, not formed into words, nor spaced in any mode. Both parents pored over them till they ascertained the letters were poetical explanations, in metre and rhyme, of the picture on the reverse. The little books were carefully put away as literary curiosities. Not long after this, Lucretia came running to her mother, painfully agitated, her face covered with her hands, and tears trickling down between her slender fingers. "O mamma! mamma!" she cried, sobbing, "how could you treat me so? You have not used me well! My little books! you have shown them to papa — Anne — Eliza; I know you have. O, what shall I do?" Her mother pleaded guilty, and .

15

tried to soothe the child by promising not to do so again : Lucretia's face brightened ; a sunny smile played through her tears as she replied, " O mamma, I am not afraid you will do so again, for I have burned them all ;" and so she had ! This reserve proceeded from nothing cold or exclusive in her character ; never was there a more loving or sympathetic creature. It would be difficult to say which was most rare, her modesty, or the genius it sanctified. She did not learn to write till she was between six and seven ; her passion for knowledge was then rapidly developing ; she read with the closest attention, and was continually running to her parents with questions and remarks that startled them. At a very early age, her mother implanted the seeds of religion, the first that should be sown in the virgin soil of the heart. That the dews of Heaven fell upon them, is evident from the breathing of piety throughout her poetry, and still more from its precious fruit in her life. Her mother remarks, that, " from her earliest years, she evinced a fear of doing anything displeasing in the sight of God ; and if, in her gayest sallies, she caught a look of disapprobation from me, she would ask, with the most artless simplicity, ' O mother, was that wicked ? ' "

There are very early, in most children's lives, certain conventional limits to their humanity, only certain forms of animal life that are respected and cherished. A robin, a butterfly, or a kitten is a legitimate object of their love and caresses ; but woe to the beetle, the caterpillar, or the rat that is thrown upon their tender mercies ! Lucretia Davidson made no such artificial discriminations ; she seemed to have an instinctive kindness for every living thing. When she was about nine, one of her school-fellows gave her a young rat that had broken its leg in attempting to escape from a trap ; she tore off a part of her pocket-handkerchief, bound up the maimed leg, carried the animal home, and nursed it tenderly. The rat, in spite of the care of its little leech, died, and was buried in the garden, and honored with the meed of a "melodious tear." This lament has not been preserved ; but one she wrote soon after, on the death of a maimed pet robin, is given here as the earliest record of her Muse that has been preserved : —

"ON THE DEATH OF MY ROBIN.

Underneath this turf doth lie
A little bird which ne'er could fly ;
Twelve large angle-worms did fill
This little bird, whom they did kill.
Puss, if you should chance to smell
My little bird from his dark cell,
O ! do be merciful, my cat,
And not serve him as you did my rat ! "

Her application to her studies at school was intense. Her mother judiciously, but in vain, attempted a diversion in favor of that legitimate sedative to female genius, the needle ; Lucretia performed her prescribed tasks with fidelity and with amazing celerity, and was again buried in her book.

When she was about twelve, she accompanied her father to the celebration of Washington's birth-night. The music and decorations excited her imagination ; but it was not with her, as with most children, the mere pleasure of stimulated sensations ; she had studied the character and history of the Father of her country, and the "fête" stirred up her enthusiasm, and inspired that feeling of actual existence and presence peculiar to minds of her temperament.

To the imaginative there is an extension of life far back into the dim past, and forward into the untried future, denied to those of common mould.

The day after the fête her elder sister found her absorbed in writing. She had sketched an urn, and written two stanzas beneath it : she was persuaded to show them to her mother ; she brought them, blushing and trembling ; her mother was ill, in bed ; but she expressed her delight with such unequivocal animation, that the child's face changed from doubt to rapture, and she seized the paper, ran away, and immediately added the concluding stanzas ; when they were finished, her mother pressed her to her bosom, wept with delight, and promised her all the aid and encouragement she could give her ; the sensitive child burst into tears. "And do you wish me to write, mamma? and will papa approve? and will it be right that I should do so ?" This delicate conscientiousness gives an imperishable charm to the stanzas, which will be found among the poems in this volume, under the title of "A Hero's Dust."

Lucretia did not escape the common trial of precocious genius. A literary friend, to whom Mrs. Davidson showed the stanzas, suspected the child had, perhaps unconsciously, repeated something she had gathered from the mass of her reading, and she betrayed her suspicion to Lucretia; she felt her rectitude impeached, and this, and not the wounded pride of the young author, made her weep till she was actually ill. As soon as she recovered her tranquillity, she offered a poetic and playful remonstrance, which set the matter at rest, and put an end to all future question of the authenticity of her productions. Before she was twelve years old, she had read the English poets. "The English poets," says Southey, in his review of Miss Davidson's poems, " though a vague term, was a wholesome course, for such a mind." She had read, beside, much history, sacred and profane, novels, and other works of imagination. Dramatic works were particularly attractive to her; her devotion to Shakspeare is expressed in an address to him written about this time, from which we extract the following stanzas : —

"Heaven, in compassion to man's erring heart,
Gave thee of virtue, then of vice a part,
Lest we, in wonder, here should bow before thee,
Break God's commandment, worship and adore thee."

Ordinary romances, and even those highly wrought fictions that without any type in Nature have such a mischievous charm for most imaginative young persons, she instinctively rejected; her healthy appetite, keen as it was, was under the government of a pure and sound nature. Her mother, always aware of the worth of the gem committed to her keeping, amidst her sufferings from ill health kept a watchful eye on her child, directed her pursuits, and sympathized in all her little school labors and trials; she perceived that Lucretia was growing pale and sickly over her studies, and she judiciously withdrew her, for a time, from school. She was soon rewarded for this wise measure by hearing her child's bounding step as she approached her sick-room, and seeing the cheek bent over her pillow blooming with returning health. How miserably mistaken are those, who fancy that all the child's lessons must be learned from the school-book and school-room! This apt pupil of Nature had only changed her books and her master; now, she sat at the feet of the great teacher, Nature, and read, and listened, and thought, as she wandered along the Saranac, or contemplated the varying aspects of Cumberland Bay. She would sit for hours and watch the progress of a thunder-storm, from the first gathering of the clouds to the farewell smile of the rainbow. "Twilight," and "The Evening Spirit," are examples of the impression of these studies and pensive meditations.

In her thirteenth year the clouds seemed heavily gathering over her morning; her mother, who had hitherto been her guide and companion, could no longer extend to her child the sympathy and encouragement which she needed. Lucretia was oppressed with the apprehension of losing this fond parent, who for weeks and months seemed upon the verge of the grave. There are, among her unpublished poems, some touching lines to her mother, written, I believe, about this time, concluding thus :—-

> "Hang not thy harp upon the willow,
>   That weeps o'er every passing wave;
> This life is but a restless pillow;
>   There's calm and peace beyond the grave."

As Mrs. Davidson's health gradually amended, with it returned her desire to give her daughter every means in her power to aid the development of her extraordinary genius. Her extreme sensibility and delicate health subjected her, at times, to depressions of spirit; but she had nothing of the morbid dejection, the exclusiveness, and hostility to the world, that are the results of self-exaggeration, selfishness, and self-idolatry, and not the natural offspring of genius and true feeling, which, in their healthy state, are pure and living fountains flowing out in abundant streams of love and kindness.

Indulgent as Mrs. Davidson was, she was too wise to permit Lucretia to forego entirely the customary employments of her sex. When engaged with these, it seems, she sometimes played truant with the Muse. Once she had promised to do a sewing task, and had eagerly run off for her work-basket; she loitered, and when she returned, she found her mother had done the work, and that there was a shade of just displeasure on her countenance. "O mamma!" she said, "I did forget; I am grieved, I did not mean to neglect you." "Where have you been, Lucretia?" "I have been writing," she replied, confused; "as I passed the window, I saw a solitary sweet pea; I thought they were all gone. This was alone; I ran to smell it; but before I could reach it, a gust of wind broke the stem. I turned away disappointed, and was coming back to you; but as I passed the table, there stood the inkstand, and I forgot you." If our readers will turn to her printed poems, and read the "Last Flower of the Garden," they will not wonder that her mother kissed her, and bade her never resist a similar impulse.

When in her "happy moments," as she termed them, the impulse to write was irresistible ; she always wrote rapidly, and sometimes expressed a wish that she had two pairs of hands, to record as fast as she composed. She wrote her short pieces standing, often three or four in a day, in the midst of the family, blind and deaf to all around her, wrapt in her own visions. She herself describes these visitations of her Muse, in an address to her, beginning —

> " Enchanted when thy voice I hear,
> I drop each earthly care ;
> I feel as wafted from the world
> To Fancy's realms of air."

When composing her long and complicated poems, like " Amir Khan," she required entire seclusion ; if her pieces were seen in the process of production, the spell was dissolved ; she could not finish them, and they were cast aside as rubbish. When writing a poem of considerable length, she retired to her own apartment, closed the blinds, and in warm weather placed her Æolian harp in the window. Her mother has described her on one of these occasions, when an artist would have painted her as a young genius communing with her Muse. We quote her mother's graphic description : " I entered the room ; she was sitting with scarcely light enough to discern the characters she was tracing ; her harp was in the window, touched by a breeze just sufficient to rouse the spirit of harmony ;

her comb had fallen on the floor, and her long dark ringlets hung in rich profusion over her neck and shoulders ; her cheek glowed with animation ; her lips were half unclosed ; her full dark eye was radiant with the light of genius, and beaming with sensibility ; her head rested on her left hand, while she held her pen in her right ; she looked like the inhabitant of another sphere ; she was so wholly absorbed that she did not observe my entrance. I looked over her shoulder and read the following lines : —

> " ' What heavenly music strikes my ravished ear,
> So soft, so melancholy, and so clear ?
> And do the tuneful Nine then touch the lyre,
> To fill each bosom with poetic fire ?
> Or does some angel strike the sounding strings
> Who caught from Echo the wild note he sings ?
> But ah ! another strain, how sweet, how wild !
> Now rushing low, 'tis soothing, soft, and mild.'

"The noise I made on leaving the room roused her, and she soon after brought me her 'Lines to an Æolian Harp.' "

During the winter of 1822 she wrote a poetical romance, entitled "Rodri." She burned this, save a few fragments found after her death. These indicate a well-contrived story, and are marked by the marvelous ease and grace that characterized her versification. During this winter she wrote also a tragedy, "The Reward of Ambition," the only production she ever read aloud to her family. The following summer, her health again failing, she was withdrawn once more from school, and sent on a visit to some friends in Canada. A letter, too long to be inserted here entire, gives a very interesting account of the impression produced on this little thoughtful and feeling recluse, by new objects and new aspects of society. "We visited," says the writer, "the British fortifications at Isle-aux-Noix. The broad ditch, the lofty ramparts, the draw-bridge, the covered gate-way, the wide-mouthed cannon, the arsenal, and all the imposing paraphernalia of a military fortress, seemed connected in her mind with powerful associations of what she had read, but never viewed before. Instead of shrinking from objects associated with carnage and death, like many who possess not half her sensibility, she appeared for the moment to be attended by the god of war, and drank the spirit of battles and siege, with the bright vision before her eyes, of conquering heroes, and wreaths of victory." It is curious to see thus early the effect of story and song in overcoming the instincts of nature; to see this tender, gentle creature contemplating the engines of war, not with natural dread as instruments of torture and death, but rather as the forges by which triumphal cars and wreaths of victory were to be wrought. A similar manifestation of the effect of tradition and association on her poetic imagination is described in the following passages from the same letter: "She found much less in the Protestant than in the Catholic churches to awaken those romantic and poetic associations, created by the record of events in the history of antiquity and traditional story, and much less to accord with the fictions of her high-wrought imagination. In viewing the buildings of the city, or the paintings in the churches, the same uniformity of taste was observable. The modern, however beautiful in design or execution, had little power to fix her attention; while the grand, the ancient, the romantic, seized upon her imagination with irresistible power. The sanctity of time seemed, to her mind, to give a sublimity to the simplest objects; and whatever was connected with great events in history, or with the lapse of ages long gone by, riveted and absorbed every faculty of her mind. During our visit to the nunneries she said but little, and seemed abstracted in thought, as if, as she herself so beautifully expresses it, to

> " ' Roll back the tide of time, and raise
> The faded forms of other days.'

"She had an opportunity of viewing an elegant collection of paintings. She seemed in ecstasies all the evening, and every feature beamed with joy." The writer, after proceeding to give an account of her surprising success in attempts at pencil-sketches from Nature, expresses his delight and amazement at the attainments of this girl of fourteen years in general literature, and at the independence and originality of mind that resisted the subduing, and, if I may be allowed the expression, the subordinating effect of this early intimacy with captivating models. A marvelous resistance, if we take into the account "that timid, retiring modesty," which, as the writer of the letter says, "marked her even to painful excess." Lucretia returned to her mother with renovated health, and her mind bright with new impressions and joyous emotions.

Religion is the natural, and only sustaining element of such a character. Where, but at the ever fresh, sweet, and life-giving fountains of the Bible, could such a spirit have drunk, and not again thirsted? During the winter of 1823, she applied herself more closely than ever to her studies. She read the Holy Scriptures with fixed attention. She almost committed to memory the Psalms of David, the Lamentations of Jeremiah, and the book of Job, guided in her selection by her poetic taste. Byron somewhere pronounces the book of Job the sublimest poetry on record. During the winter Miss Davidson wrote "A Hymn on Creation," "The Exit from Egyptian Bondage," and versified many chapters of the Bible. She read the New Testament, and particularly those parts of it that contained the most affecting passages in the history of our Saviour, with the deepest emotion.

In her intellectual pursuits and attainments only was she premature. She retained unimpared the innocence, simplicity, and modesty of a child. We have had descriptions of the extreme loveliness of her face, and gracefulness of her person, from less doubtful authority than a fond mother.

Our country towns are not regulated by the conventional systems of the cities, where a youthful beauty is warily confined to the nursery and the school till the prescribed age for *coming out*, the *coup-de-theatre* of every young city-woman's life, arrives. In the country, as soon as a girl can contribute to the pleasures of society, she is invited into it. During the winter of 1823, Plattsburgh was gay, and Miss Davidson was eagerly

sought to embellish the village dances. She had been
at a dancing school, and, like most young persons, enjoyed excessively this natural exercise; for that may be
called natural which exists among all nations, barbarous
and civilized.

Mrs. Davidson has given an account of her daughter's
first ball, which all young ladies, at least, will thank us
for transcribing almost verbatim, as it places her more
within the circle of their sympathies. Her mother had
consented to her attending one or two public assemblies,
in the hope they might diminish her extreme timid-
ity, painful both to Lucretia and her friends. The day
arrived; Mrs. Davidson was consulting with her eldest
daughter upon the all-important matter of the dresses
for the evening; Lucretia sat by, reading, without raising her eyes from the book, one of the Waverly Novels.
"Mamma, what shall Luly wear?" asked her eldest sister, calling her by the pretty diminutive by which they
usually addressed her at home. "Come, Lucretia, what
color will you wear to-night?" "Where?" "Where;
why, to the assembly, to be sure." "The assembly; is it
to-night? so it is!" and she tossed away the book and
danced about the room half wild with delight; her sister
at length called her to order, and the momentous question respecting the dress was definitely settled; she then
resumed her reading, and, giving no thought to the ball,
she was again absorbed in her book. This did not result from carelessness of appearance, or indifference to
dress; on the contrary, she was rather remarkable for
that nice taste which belongs to an eye for proportion
and coloring; and any little embellishment or ornament

she wore was well chosen and well placed; but she had the right estimate of the relative value of objects, which belongs to a superior mind. When the evening approached, the star of the ball again shone forth; she threw aside her book, and began the offices of the toilet with girlish interest, and, it might be, some heart-beating at the probable effect of the lovely face her mirror reflected. Her sister was to arrange her hair. Lucretia put on her dressing-gown to await her convenience; but when the time came, she was missing. "We called her in vain," says Mrs. Davidson; "at last, opening the parlor door, I distinctly saw, for it was twilight, some person sitting behind the large close stove; I approached, and found Lucretia writing poetry! moralizing on what the world calls pleasure! I was almost dumb with amazement. She was eager to go, delighted with the prospect of pleasure before her; yet she acted as if the time were too precious to spend in the necessary preparations, and she sat still, and finished the last stanza, while I stood by, mute with astonishment at this strange bearing in a girl of fourteen, preparing to attend her first ball, an event she had anticipated with so many mingled emotions." "She returned from the assembly," continues her mother, "wild with delight. 'O mamma,' she said, 'I wish you had been there! when I first entered, the glare of light dazzled my eyes; my head whirled, and I felt as if I were treading on air; all was so gay, so brilliant! but I grew tired at last, and was glad to hear sister say it was time to go home.'"

The next day the ball was dismissed from her mind, and she returned to her studies with her customary ardor. During the winter she read " Josephus," " Charles the Fifth," " Charles Twelfth ;" read over " Shakspeare," and various other works in prose and poetry ; she particularly liked " Addison," and read almost every day a portion of the " Spectator." Her ardent love of literature seldom interfered with her social dispositions, *never* with her domestic affections ; she was ever the life and joy of the home circle. Great demands were made on her feelings about this time, by two extraordinary domestic events, — the marriage and removal of her elder sister, her beloved friend and companion, and the birth of another, the little Margaret, so often the fond subject of her poetry. New and doubtless sanative emotions were called forth by this last event. The lines entitled " On the Birth of a Sister," were written about this time ; and " The Smile of Innocence," marked, we think, by more originality and beauty, were written soon after, and, as the previously mentioned ones were, with her infant sister in her lap. What a subject for a painter would this beautiful impersonation of genius and love have presented !

The last three most beautiful stanzas, which we here quote, must have been inspired by the sleeping infant on her lap, and they seem to have reflected her soul's image, as we have seen the little inland lake catch and give back the marvelous beauty of the sunset clouds.

> " But there's a smile, 't is sweeter still,
>   'Tis one far dearer to my soul ;
> It is a smile which angels might
>   Upon their brightest list enroll.

"It is the smile of innocence,
    Of sleeping infancy's light dream;
Like lightning on a summer's eve,
    It sheds a soft and pensive gleam.

"It dances round the dimpled cheek,
    And tells of happiness within;
It smiles what it can never speak, —
    A human heart devoid of sin."

"Soon after her marriage," says Mrs. Davidson, "her sister, Mrs. Townsend, removed to Canada; and many circumstances combined to interrupt her literary pursuits, and call forth, not only the energies of her mind but to develop the filial devotion and total sacrifice of all selfish feelings, which gave a new and elevated tone to her character, and showed us that there was no gratification, either in pursuance of mental improvement, or personal ease, but must bend to her high standard of filial duty." Her mother was very ill, and to add to the calamity, her monthly nurse was taken sick, and left her; the infant, too, was ill. Lucretia sustained her multiplied cares with firmness and efficiency: the conviction that she was doing her duty gave her strength almost preternatural. I shall again quote her mother's words, for I fear to enfeeble, by any version of my own, the beautiful example of this conscientious little being. "Lucretia astonished us all; she took her station in my sick-room, and devoted herself wholly to the mother and the child; and when my recovery became doubtful, instead of resigning herself to grief, her exertions were redoubled, not only for the comfort of the sick, but she was an angel of consolation to her afflicted father. We were amazed at the exertions she made, and the fatigue she endured; for, with nerves so weak, a constitution so delicate, and sensibility so exquisite, we trembled lest she should sink with anxiety and fatigue. Until it ceased to be necessary, she performed not only the duty of a nurse, but acted as superintendent of the household." When her mother became convalescent, Lucretia continued her attentions to domestic affairs. " She did not so much yield to her ruling passion as to look into a book, or take up a pen (says her mother) lest she should again become so absorbed in them as to neglect to perform those little offices which a feeble, affectionate mother had a right to claim at her hands." As was to be expected from the intimate union of soul and body, when her mind was starved, it became dejected and her body weak; and, in spite of her filial efforts, her mother detected tears on her cheeks, was alarmed by her excessive paleness, and expressed her apprehensions that she was ill. " No, mamma," she replied, " not ill, only out of spirits." Her mother then remarked that of late she never read or wrote. She burst into tears, a full explanation followed, and the generous mother succeeded in convincing her child that she had been misguided in the course she had adopted; that the strongest wish of her heart was to advance her in her literary career, and for this she would make every exertion in her power; at the same time she very judiciously advised her to intersperse her literary pursuits with those domestic occupations so essential to prepare every woman in our land for a housewife, her probable destiny.

16

This conversation had a most happy effect; the stream flowed again in its natural channel, and Lucretia became cheerful, read and wrote, and practiced drawing. She had a decided taste for drawing, and excelled in it. She sung over her work, and in every way manifested the healthy condition that results from a wise obedience to the laws of nature.

We trust there are thousands of young ladies in our land, who, at the call of filial duty, would cheerfully perform domestic labor; but if there are any who would make a strong love for more elevated and refined pursuits an excuse for neglecting these coarser duties, we would commend them to the example of this conscientious child. She, if any could, might have pleaded her genius, or her delicate health, or her mother's most tender indulgence, for a failure, that in her would have hardly seemed to us a fault.

During this summer, she went to Canada with her mother, where she reveled in an unexplored library, and enjoyed most heartily the social pleasures at her sister's. They frequently had a family concert of music in the evening. Mrs. Townsend (her sister) accompanied the instruments with her fine voice. Lucretia was often moved by the music, and particularly by her favorite song, Moore's "Farewell to my Harp;" this she would have sung to her at twilight, when it would excite a shivering through her whole frame. On one occasion, she became cold and pale, and was near fainting, and afterwards poured her excited feelings forth in the lines addressed "To my Sister."

We insert here a striking circumstance that occurred

during a visit to her sister the following year. She was at that time employed in writing her longest published poem, "Amir Khan." Immediately after breakfast she went to walk ; and not returning to dinner, nor even when the evening approached, Mr. Townsend set forth in search of her. He met her, and as her eye encountered his, she smiled and blushed, as if she felt conscious of having been a little ridiculous. She said she had called on a friend, and, having found her absent, had gone to her library, where she had been examining some volumes of an Encyclopedia to aid her, we believe, in the Oriental story she was employed upon. She forgot her dinner and her tea, and had remained reading, standing, and with her hat on, till the disappearance of daylight brought her to her senses. In the interval between her visits, she wrote several letters to her friends, which are chiefly interesting from the indications they afford of her social and affectionate spirit. We subjoin a few extracts. She had returned to Plattsburg amid the bustle of a Fourth of July celebration.

"We found," she says, "our brother Yankees had turned out well to celebrate the Fourth. The wharf, from the hill to the very edge of the water, even the rafts and sloops, were black with the crowd. If some very good genius, who presided over my destiny at that time, had not spread its protecting pinions around me, like everything else in my possession, I should have lost even my precious self. What a truly lamentable accident it would have been just at that moment! We took a carriage, and were extricating ourselves

from the crowd, when Mr. ——, who had pressed himself through, came to shake hands and bid good-
by. He is now on his way to ——. Well! here
is health, happiness, and a bushel of love to all *mar-
ried* people! Is it possible, you ask, that sister Luc
could ever have permitted such a toast to pass her
lips? We arrived safely at our good old home, and
found everything as we left it. The chimney swallows
had taken up their residence in the chimney, and rat-
tled the soot from their sable habitations over the
hearth and carpet. It looked like desolation indeed.
The grass is high in the yard; the wild-roses, double-
roses, and sweet-briers are in full bloom, and, take it all
in all, the spot looks much as the garden of Eden did
after the expulsion of Adam and Eve. We had just
done tea when M. came in and sat an hour or two.
What in the name of wonder could he have found to
talk about all that time? Something, dear sister, you
would not have thought of; something of so little consequence that the time he spent glided swiftly, almost
unnoticed. I had him all to myself, tête-à-tête. I had
almost forgotten to tell you I had yesterday a present
of a most beautiful bouquet: I wore it to church in the
afternoon; but it has withered and faded, —

> ' Withered, like the world's treasures,
> Faded, like the world's pleasures.' "

From the sort of mystical, girl-like allusions in the
above extracts, to persons whose initials only are given,
to bouquets and tête-à-têtes, we infer that she thus early
had declared lovers even at this age, for she was not

yet sixteen: her mother says she had resolved never
to marry. "Her reasons," continues her mother, "for
this decision were, that her peculiar habits, her entire
devotion to her books, and scribbling (as she called it)
unfitted her for the care of a family; she could not do
justice to husband or children, while her whole soul
was absorbed in literary pursuits; she was not willing
to resign them for any man; therefore she had formed
the resolution to lead a single life," — a resolution that
would have lasted probably till she had passed under
the dominion of a stronger passion than her love for
the Muses. With affections like hers, and a most
lovely person and attractive manners, her resolution
would scarcely have enabled her to escape the common
destiny of her sex. The following is an extract from a
letter written after participating in several gay parties:
" Indeed, my dear brother, I have turned round like a
top for the last two or three weeks, and am glad to
seat myself once more in my favorite corner. How,
think you, should I stand it to be whirled in the giddy
round of dissipation? I come home from the blaze of
light, from the laugh of mirth, the smile of complai-
sance, and seeming happiness, and the vision passes
from my mind like the brilliant but transitory hues of
the rainbow; and I think with regret on the many,
very many happy hours I have passed with you and
Annie. O! I do want to see you, indeed I do. You
think me wild, thoughtless, and perhaps unfeeling;
but I assure you I can be sober. I sometimes think,
and I can and do feel. Why have you not written?
not one word in almost three weeks! Dear brother

and sister, I must write; but, dear Annie, I am now doomed to dim your eye and cloud your brow, for I know that what I have to communicate will surprise and distress you. Our dear cousin John is dead! O! I need not tell you how much, how deeply he is lamented; you knew him, and like every one else who did, you loved him. Poor Eliza! how my heart aches for her! her father, her mother, her brother, all gone; almost the last, the dearest tie is broken which bound her to life; what a vacancy must there be in her heart! How fatal would it prove to almost every hope in life, were we allowed even a momentary glimpse of futurity! for often half the enjoyments of life consist in the anticipation of pleasures, which may never be ours." Soon after this Lucretia witnessed the death of a beloved young friend; it was the first death she had seen, and it had its natural effect on a reflecting and sensitive mind. Her thoughts wandered through eternity by the light of religion, the only light that penetrates beyond the death-bed. She wrote many religious pieces, — and among them one commencing with

" O that the eagle's wing were mine."

During this winter her application to her books was so unremitting that her parents again became alarmed for her health, and persuaded her occasionally to join in the amusements of Plattsburg. She came home one night at twelve o'clock, from a ball; and, after giving a most lively account of all she had seen and heard to her mother, she quietly seated herself at the table, and wrote her " Reflections after leaving a Ball-room." Her spirit, though it glided with kind sympathies into the common pleasures of youth, never seemed to relax its tie to the spiritual world.

During the summer of 1824, Captain Partridge visited Plattsburg, with his soldier scholars. Military display had its usual exciting effect on Miss Davidson's imagination, and she addressed to the "Vermont Cadets" several spirited stanzas, which might have come from the martial Clorinda.

It was about this time that she finished "Amir Khan," and began a tale of some length, which she entitled the "Recluse of the Saranac." "Amir Khan" has long been before the public; but we think it has suffered from a general and very natural distrust of precocious genius. The versification is graceful, the story beautifully developed, and the Orientalism well sustained. We think it would not have done discredit to our best popular poets in the meridian of their fame: as the production of a girl of fifteen, it seems prodigious. On her mother discovering and reading a part of her romance, Lucretia manifested her usual shrinkings, and with many tears exacted a promise that she would not again look at it till it was finished; she never again saw it till after her daughter's death. Lucretia had a most whimsical fancy for cutting sheets of paper into narrow strips, sewing them together, and writing on both sides; and once playfully boasting to her mother of having written some yards, she produced a roll, and forbidding her mother's approach, she measured off twenty yards! She often expressed a wish to spend one fortnight alone, even to the exclusion of her little pet sister; and Mrs. Davidson,

eager to afford her every gratification in her power, had
a room prepared for her recess ; her dinner was sent up
to her, she declined coming down to tea, and her mother,
on going to her apartment, found her writing, — her
plate untouched.

Some secret joy it was natural her mother should feel
at this devotion to intellectual pleasure ; but her good
sense or her maternal anxiety got the better of it, and
she persuaded Lucretia to consent to the interruption of
a daily walk. It was about this period that she became
acquainted with the gentleman who was destined to influence the brief space of life that remained to her.
The late Hon. Moss Kent, with whom her mother had
been acquainted for many years previous to her marriage, had often been a guest at the house of Dr. Davidson, but it had so happened that he had never met Lucretia since her early childhood. Struck with some little
effusions which were in the possession of his sister, Mrs.
P——, he went immediately to see Mrs. Davidson, to
ask the privilege of reading some of her last productions.
On his way to the house he met Lucretia ; he had been
interested by the reputation of her genius and modesty ;
no wonder that the beautiful form in which it was en-
shrined, should have called this interest into sudden and
effective action. Miss Davidson was just sixteen ; her
complexion was the most beautiful brunette, clear and
brilliant, of that warm tint that seems to belong to lands
of the sun rather than to our chilled regions ; indeed,
her whole organization, mental as well as physical, her
deep and quick sensibility, her early development, were
characteristics of a warmer clime than ours ; her stature

was of the middle height, her form slight and symmetrical, her hair profuse, dark, and curling, her mouth and nose regular, and as beautiful as if they had been chiseled by an inspired artist; and through this fitting medium beamed her angelic spirit. "Mr. Kent, with all the enthusiasm inherent in his nature, after examining her commonplace-book, resolved, if he could induce her parents to resign Lucretia to his care, to afford her every facility for improvement that could be obtained in the country; and in short, he proposed to adopt her as his own child. Her parents took the subject into consideration, and complied so far with his benevolent wishes as to permit him to take an active interest in her education, deferring to future consideration the question of his adopting her. Had she lived, they would, no doubt, have consented to his plan. It was, after some deliberation, decided to send her a few months to the Troy Seminary; and on the same evening she wrote the following letter to her brother and sister : —

"What think you? 'ere another moon shall fill, round as my shield,' I shall be at Mrs. Willard's seminary; in a fortnight I shall probably have left Plattsburg, not to return at least until the expiration of six months. O! I am so delighted, so happy! I shall scarcely eat, drink, or sleep for a month to come. You and Anne must both write to me often; and you must not laugh when you think of poor Luly in the far-famed city of Troy, dropping handkerchiefs, keys, gloves, etc.; in short, something of everything I have. It is well if you can read what I have written, for papa and mamma are talking, and my head whirls like a top. O! how my poor head aches! Such a surprise as I have had!"

On the 24th of November, 1824, she left home, health
on her cheek and in her bosom, and flushed with the
most ardent expectations of getting rapidly forward in
the career her desires were fixed upon. But even at
this moment her fond devotion to her mother was beautifully expressed, in some stanzas which she left where
they would meet her eye as soon as the parting tears
were wiped away. These stanzas are already published,
and I shall only quote two from them, striking for their
tenderness and truth.

> " To thee my lay is due, the simple song
>   Which nature gave me at life's opening day ;
> To thee these rude, these untaught strains belong,
>   Whose heart, indulgent, will not spurn my lay !
>
> " O say, amid this wilderness of life
>   What bosom would have throbbed like thine for me ?
> Who would have smiled responsive ? Who in grief
>   Would e'er have felt, and, feeling, grieved like thee ? "

The following extracts from her letters, which were
always filled with yearnings for home, will show that her
affections were the stronghold of her nature : —

" *Troy Seminary, December 6th*, 1824. — Here I am at
last ; and what a naughty girl I was, when I was at
Aunt Schuyler's, that I did not write you everything !
But to tell the truth, I was topsy-turvy, and so I am now ;
but in despite of calls from the young ladies, and of a
hundred new faces, and new names which are constantly
ringing in my ears, I have set myself down, and will not
rise until I have written an account of everything to my
dear mother. I am contented ; yet, notwithstanding, I
have once or twice turned a wishful glance towards my

dear-loved home. Amidst all the parade of wealth, in the splendid apartments of luxury, I can assure you, my dearest mother, that I had rather be with you *in our own lovely home* than in the midst of all this ceremony."

"O mamma, I like Mrs. Willard. 'And so this is my girl, Mrs. Schuyler?' said she, and took me affectionately by the hand. O, I want to see you so much! But I must not think of it now. I must learn as fast as I can, and think only of my studies. Dear, dear little Margaret! kiss her and the little boys for me. How is dear father getting on in this rattling world?"

The letters that followed were tinged with melancholy from her "bosom's depth," and her mother has withheld them. In a subsequent one she says, "I have written two long letters; but I wrote when I was ill, and they savor too much of sadness. I feel a little better now, and have again commenced my studies. Mr. K. called here to-day. O, he is very good! He stayed some time, and brought a great many books; but I fear I shall have little time to read aught but what appertains to my studies. I am consulting Kames's 'Elements of Criticism,' studying French, attending to geological lectures, composition, reading, paying some little attention to painting, and learning to dance."

A subsequent letter indicated great unhappiness and debility, and awakened her mother's apprehensions. The next was written more cheerfully. "As I fly to you," she says, "for consolation in all my sorrows, so I turn to you, my dear mother, to participate in all my joys. The clouds that enveloped my mind have dispersed, and I turn to you with a far lighter heart than

when I last wrote.   The ever kind Mr. K. called yesterday."   She then describes the paternal interest he took
in her health and happiness, expresses a trembling apprehension lest he should be disappointed in the amount
of her improvement, and laments the loss of time from
her frequent indisposition.   " How, my dear mother,"
she says, " shall I express my gratitude to my kind, my
excellent friend ?   What is felt as deeply as I feel this
obligation, *cannot* be expressed : but I can feel, and *do*
feel."   It must be remembered that these were not for-
mal and obligatory letters to her guardian, but the spontaneous overflowing of her heart in her private corre-
spondence with her mother.

"We now begin to dread the examination.   O, hor-
rible ! seven weeks, and I shall be posted up before
all Troy, all the students from Schenectady, and perhaps five hundred others.   What shall I do?

" I have just received a note from Mr. K., in which
he speaks of your having written to him of my illness.
I was indeed ill, and very ill, for several days, and in
my deepest dejection wrote to you ; but do not, my
dearest mother, be alarmed about me.   My appetite is
not perfectly good, but quite as well as when I was
at home.   The letter was just such a one as was cal-
culated to soothe my feelings, and set me completely
at rest.   He expressed a wish that my stay here should
be prolonged.   What think you, mother ?   I should be
delighted by such an arrangement.   This place really
seems quite like home to me, though not *my own
dear home.*   I like Mrs. Willard, I love the girls, and
I have the vanity to think I am not actually disagree-
able to them."

We come now to another expression (partly serious and partly bantering, for she seems to have uniformly respected her instructress) of her terrors of "examination."

"We are engaged, heart and hand, preparing for this awful examination. O, how I dread it! But there is no retreat. I must stand firm to my post, or experience all the anger, vengeance, and punishments, which will, in case of delinquency or flight, be exercised with the most unforgiving acrimony. We are in such cases excommunicated, henceforth and forever, under the awful ban of holy Seminary; and the evil eye of false report is upon us. O mamma, I do, though, jesting apart, dread this examination; but nothing short of real and absolute sickness can excuse a scholar in the eyes of Mrs. Willard. Even that will not do it to the Trojan world around us; for if a young lady is ill at examination, they say, with a sneer, 'O, she is ill of an examination fever!' Thus you see, mamma, we have no mercy either from friends or foes. We must '*do or die.*' Tell Morris he must write to me. Kiss dear, dear little Margaret for me, and don't let her forget *poor sister Luly*, and tell all who inquire for me that I am well, but in awful dread of a great examination."

The following extract is from a letter to her friends, who had written under the impression that all letters received by the young ladies were, of course, read by some one of the officers of the institution: —

"Lo! just as I was descending from the third story (for you must know I hold my head high), your letter was put into my hands. Poor little wanderer! I really felt a sisterly compassion for the poor little folded paper. I kissed it for the sake of those who sent it forth into the wide world, and put it into my bosom. But O. when I read it! Now, Anne, I will tell you the truth; it was cold; perhaps it was written on one of your cold Canada days, or perchance it lost a little heat on the way. It did not seem to come from the very heart of hearts; it looked as though it were written 'to a young lady at the Troy Seminary,' not to your dear, dear, *dear sister Luly*. Mr. K. has thus far been a father to me, and I thank him; but I will not mock my feelings by attempting to say how much I thank him."

"My dear mother! O how I wish I could lay my head upon your bosom! I hope you do not keep my letters, for I certainly have burned all yours;* and I stood like a little fool and wept over their ashes; and when I saw the last one gone, I felt as though I had parted with my last friend." Then, after expressing an earnest wish that her mother would destroy her letters, she says, "They have no connection. When I write, everything comes crowding upon me at once; my pen moves too slow for my brain and my heart, and I feel vexed at myself, and tumble in everything together, and a choice medley you have of it!

"I attended Mr. Ball's public (assembly) last night, and had a delightful evening; but now for something of more importance, — *Ex-am-i-na-tion!* I had just begun to be engaged, heart and hand, preparing for it, when, by some means, I took a violent cold. I was unable to raise my voice above a whisper, and coughed incessantly.

---

* This was in consequence of a positive command from her mother.

On the second day, Mrs. Willard sent for Dr. Robbins ; he said I must be bled, and take an emetic ; this was sad ; but, O mamma, I could not speak or breathe without pain." There are further details of pains, remedies, and consequent exhaustion ; and yet this fragile and precious creature was permitted by her physician and friends, kind and watchful friends too, to proceed in her suicidal preparations for examination ! There was nothing uncommon in this injudiciousness. Such violations of the laws of our physical nature are every day committed by persons in other respects the wisest and the best ; and our poor little martyr may not have suffered in vain, if her experience awakens attention to the subject.

In the letter from which we have quoted above, and which is filled with expressions of love for the dear ones at home, she continues : " Tell Morris I will answer his letter in full next quarter ; but now I fear I am doing wrong, for I am yet quite feeble ; and when I get stronger, I shall be very avaricious of my time, in order to prepare for the coming week.

" We must study morning, noon, and night. *I shall rise between two and four now every morning, till the dreaded day is past.* I rose the other night at twelve, but was ordered back to bed again. You see, mamma, I shall have a chance to become an early riser here." " Had I not written you that I was coming home, I think I should not have seen you this winter. All my friends think I had better remain here, as the journey will be long and cold ; but O ! there is that at the journey's end which would tempt me through the wilds of

Siberia, — father, mother, brothers, sisters, *home.*   Yes, I shall come."

We insert some stanzas written about this time, not so much for their poetical merit as for the playful spirit that beams through them, and which seems like sunbeams smiling on a cataract.

A WEEK BEFORE EXAMINATION.

One has a headache, one a cold,
One has her neck in flannel rolled ;
Ask the complaint, and you are told,
          " Next week's examination."

One frets and scolds, and laughs and cries ;
Another hopes, despairs, and sighs ;
Ask but the cause, and each replies,
          " Next week's examination."

One bans her books, then grasps them tight,
And studies morning, noon, and night,
As though she took some strange delight
          In these examinations.

The books are marked, defaced, and thumbed,
The brains with midnight tasks benumbed,
Still all in that account is summed,
          " Next week's examination."

In a letter, February 10th, she says, " The dreaded work of examination is now going on, my dear mother. To-morrow evening, which will be the last, and is always the most crowded, is the time fixed upon for my *entrée* upon the field of action.   O ! I hope I shall not disgrace myself.   It is the rule here to reserve the best classes till the last ; so I suppose I may take it as a compliment that we are delayed."

" February 12th. — The examination is over. E——
E—— did herself and her native village honor ; but as
for your poor Luly, she acquitted herself, I trust, de-
cently ! O mamma, I was so frightened ! but, although
my face glowed and my voice trembled, I did make out
to get through, for I knew my lessons. The room was
crowded almost to suffocation. All was still, — the fall
of a pin could have been heard, — and I tremble when I
think of it even now." No one can read these melancholy records without emotion.

Her visit home during the vacation was given up, in
compliance with the advice of her guardian. " I wept a
good long hour or so," she says, with her characteristic
gentle acquiescence, " and then made up my mind to be
content."

In her next letter she relates an incident very striking
in her eventful life.

It occurred in returning to Troy, after her vacation,
passed happily with her friends in the vicinity. " Uncle
went to the ferry with me," she says, " where we met
Mr. Paris. Uncle placed me under his care, and, snugly
seated by his side, I expected a very pleasant ride with
a very pleasant gentleman. All was pleasant, except
that we expected every instant that all the ice in the
Hudson would come drifting against us, and shut in
scow, stage, and all, or sink us to the bottom, which, in
either case, you know, mother, would not have been
quite so agreeable. We had just pushed from the shore,
I watching the ice with anxious eyes, when, lo ! the two
leaders made a tremendous plunge, and tumbled headlong into the river. I felt the carriage following fast

after ; the other two horses pulled back with all their power, but the leaders were dragging them down, dashing and plunging, and flouncing in the water. ' Mr. Paris, in mercy let us get out !' said I. But, as he did not see the horses, he felt no alarm. The moment I informed him they were overboard, he opened the door, and cried, ' Get out and save yourself, if possible ; I am old and stiff, but I will follow in an instant.' ' Out with the lady ! let the lady out !' shouted several voices at once ; ' the other horses are about to plunge, and then all will be over.' I made a lighter spring than many a lady does in a cotillon, and jumped upon a cake of ice. Mr. Paris followed, and we stood (I trembling like a leaf) expecting every instant that the next plunge of the drowning horses would detach the piece of ice upon which we were standing, and send us adrift ; but, thank Heaven, after working for ten or fifteen minutes, by dint of ropes, and cutting them away from the other horses, they dragged the poor creatures out, more dead than alive.

" Mother, don't you think I displayed some courage ? I jumped into the stage again, and shut the door, while Mr. Paris remained outside, watching the movement of affairs. We at length reached here, and I am alive, as you see, to tell the story of my woes."

In her next letter she details a conversation with Mrs. Willard, full of kind commendation and good counsel. " Mamma," she concludes, " you would be justified in thinking me a perfect lump of vanity and egotism ; but I have always related to you every thought, every action, of my life. I have had no concealments from you, and I have stated these matters to you because they fill me with surprise. Who would think the accomplished Mrs. Willard would admire my poor daubing, or my poor anything else! O dear mamma, I am so happy now! so contented! Every unusual movement startles me. I am constantly afraid of something to mar it."

The next extract is from a letter, the emanation of her affectionate spirit, to a favorite brother seven years old.

" Dear L——, I am obliged to you for your two very interesting epistles, and much doubt whether I could spell more ingeniously myself. Really, I have some idea of sending them to the printers, to be struck off in imitation of a Chinese puzzle. Your questions about the stars I have been cogitating some time past, and am of the opinion that if there are beings inhabiting those heavenly regions, they must be content to feed, chameleon-like, upon air; for even were we disposed to spare them a portion of our earth sufficient to plant a garden, I doubt whether the attraction of gravitation would not be too strong for resistance, and the unwilling clod return to its pale brethren of the valley ' to rest in ease inglorious.' So far from burning your precious letters, my dear little brother, I carefully preserve them in a little pocket-book; and when I feel lonely and desolate, and think of my dear home, I turn them over and over again. Do write often, my sweet little correspondent, and believe me," etc., etc.

Her next letter to her mother, written in March, was in a melancholy strain; but as if to avert her parent's consequent anxieties, she concludes:—

" I hope you will feel no concern for my health or happiness. Do, my dear mother, try to be cheerful, and have good courage."

"I have been to the Rensselaer school, to attend the philosophical lectures. They are delivered by the celebrated Mr. Eaton, who has several students, young gentlemen. I hope they will not lose their hearts among twenty or thirty pretty girls. For my part, I kept my eyes fixed as fast as might be upon the good old lecturer, as I am of the opinion that he is the best possible safeguard, with his philosophy and his apparatus; for you know philosophy and love are sworn enemies!"

Miss Davidson returned to Plattsburg during the spring vacation. Her mother, when the first rapture of reunion was over, the first joy at finding her child unchanged in the modesty and naturalness of her deportment, and fervor of her affections, became alarmed at the indications of disease, in the extreme fragility of her person, and the deep and fluctuating color of her cheek. Lucretia insisted, and, deceived by that ever-deceiving disease, believed she was well. She was gay and full of hope, and could hardly be persuaded to submit to her father's medical prescriptions; but the well-known crimson spot, that so often flushed her cheek, was regarded by him with the deepest anxiety, and he shortly called counsel. During her stay at home she wrote a great deal. Like the bird, which is to pass away with the summer, she seems to have been ever on the wing, pouring forth the spontaneous melodies of her soul.

The physician called in to consult with her father was of opinion that a change of air and scene would probably restore her, and it was decided, in compliance with her own wishes, that she should *return to school.*

Miss Gilbert's boarding-school, at Albany, was se-

lected for the next six months. There are few more of
her productions of any sort, and they seem to us to have
the sweetness of the last roses of summer. The following playful passages are from her last letter at home to
her sister in Canada : —

"The boat will be here in an hour or two, and I am
all ready to start. O, I am half sick. I have taken several doses of something quite delectable for a visiting
treat. Now," she concludes her letter, "by your affection for me, by your pity for the wanderer, by your re-
membrance of the absent, by your love for each other,
and by all that is sacred to an absent friend, I charge
you, write to me, and write often. As ye hope to prosper, as ye hope your boy to prosper (and grow fat !), as
ye hope for my gratitude and affection now and here-
after, I charge you write. If ye sinfully neglect this last
solemn injunction of a parting friend, my injured spirit
will visit you in your transgressions. It shall pierce you
with goose-quills, and hurl down upon your recreant
heads the brimming contents of the neglected inkstand.
This is my threat, and this is my vengeance. But if, on
the contrary, ye shall see fit to honor me with numerous
epistles, which shall be duly answered, know ye, that I
will live and love you, and not only you, but your boy !
So, you see, upon your own bearing depends the future
fate of the little innocent, 'to be beloved, or not to be
beloved !' They have come ! Farewell, a long farewell !"

She proceeded to Albany, and in a letter dated May
12th, 1825, she seems delighted with her reception, ac-
commodations, and prospects at Miss Gilbert's school.

She has yet no anxieties about her health, and enters on her career of study with her customary ardor. With the most delicate health and constant occupation, she found time always to write long letters to her mother and the little children at home, filled with fond expressions. What an example and rebuke to the idle school-girl who finds no time for these minor duties! But her studies, to which she applied herself beyond her strength, from the conscientious fear of not fulfilling the expectations of her friends, were exhausting the sources of life. Her letters teem with expressions of gratitude to her friend Mr. K., to Miss Gilbert, and to all the friends around her. She complains of debility and want of appetite, but imputes all her ailings to not hearing regularly from home. The mails were of course at fault, for her mother's devotion never intermitted. The following expressions will show that her sensibility, naturally acute, was rendered intense by physical disease and suffering.

" O my dear mother, cannot you send your Luly one line? Not one word in two weeks! I have done nothing but weep all day long. I feel so wretchedly! I am afraid you are ill.

" I am very wretched, indeed I am. My dear mother, am I never to hear from you again? I am *homesick*. I know I am *foolish;* but I cannot help it. To tell the truth, I am half sick. I am so weak, so languid, I cannot eat. I am nervous, I know I am; I weep most of the time. I have blotted the paper so, that I cannot write. I cannot study much longer, if I do not hear from you."

Letters from home renovated her for a few days; and at Mr. K.'s request, she went to the theatre, and gave herself up, with all the freshness of youthful feeling, to the spells of the drama, and raved about Hamlet and Ophelia like any other school-girl.

But her next letter recurs to her malady, and for the first time she expresses a fear that her disease is beyond the reach of common remedies. Her mother was alarmed, and would have gone immediately to her, but she was herself confined to her room by illness. Her father's cooler judgment inferred, from their receiving no letters from Lucretia's friends, that there was nothing immediately alarming in her symptoms.

The next letter removed every doubt. It was scarcely legible : still she assures her mother she is better, and begs she will not risk the consequences of a long journey. But neither health nor life weighed now with the mother against seeing her child. She set off, and, by appointment, joined Mr. K. at Whitehall. They proceeded thence to Albany, where, after the first emotions of meeting were over, Lucretia said, " O mamma, I thought I should never have seen you again ! But, now I have you here, and can lay my aching head upon your bosom, I shall soon be better."

For a few days the balm seemed effectual ; she was better, and the physicians believed she would recover ; but her mother was no longer to be persuaded from her conviction of the fatal nature of the disease, and arrangements were immediately made to convey her to Plattsburg. The journey was effected, notwithstanding it was during the heats of July, with less physical suffering than was apprehended. She shrank painfully from the gaze her beauty inevitably attracted, heightened as it was by that disease which seems to delight to deck the victim for its triumph. "Her joy upon finding herself at home," says her mother, "operated for a time like magic." The sweet health-giving influence of domestic love, the home atmosphere, seemed to suspend the progress of her disease, and again her father, brothers, and friends were deluded; all but the mother and the sufferer. She looked, with prophetic eye, calmly to the end. There was nothing to disturb her. That kingdom that cometh "without observation" was within her; and she was only about to change its external circumstances, about to put off the harness of life in which she had been so patient and obedient. To the last she manifested her love of books. A trunk filled with them had not been unpacked. She requested her mother to open it at her bedside; and as each book was given to her, she turned over the leaves, kissed it, and desired to have it placed on a table at the foot of her bed. There they remained to the last, her eye often fondly resting on them.

She expressed a strong desire to see Mr. Kent once more, and a fear that though he had been summoned, he might not arrive in time. He came, however, to receive the last expressions of her gratitude, and to hear his own name the last pronounced by her lips.

The "Fear of Madness" was written by her while confined to her bed, and was the last piece she ever wrote. It constitutes a part of the history of her disease, and will, for this reason alone, if no other, be read with interest.

That the records of the last scenes of Lucretia Davidson's life are scanty, is not surprising. The materials for this memoir, it must be remembered, were furnished by her mother. A victim stretched on the rack cannot keep records. She says, in* general terms, " Lucretia frequently spoke to me of her approaching dissolution with perfect calmness, and as an event that must soon take place. In a conversation with Mr. Townsend, held at intervals, as her strength would permit, she expressed the sentiments she expressed to me before she grew so weak. She declared her firm faith in the Christian religion, her dependence on the divine promises, which she said had consoled and sustained her during her illness. She said her hopes of salvation were grounded on the merits of her Saviour, and that death, which had once looked so dreadful to her, was now divested of all its terrors."

Welcome, indeed, should that messenger have been that opened the gates of knowledge and blissful immortality to such a spirit !

During Miss Davidson's residence in Albany, which was less than three months, she wrote several miscellaneous pieces, and began a long poem, divided into cantos, and entitled " Maritorne, or the Pirate of Mexico." This she deemed better than anything she had previously produced. The amount of her compositions, considering the shortness and multifarious occupations of a life of less than seventeen years, is surprising.

We copy the subjoined paragraph from the biographical sketch prefixed to " Amir Khan." " Her poetical writings, which have been collected, amount in all to two hundred and seventy-eight pieces, of various lengths. When it is considered that there are among these at least five regular poems, of several cantos each, some estimate may be formed of her poetical labors. Besides these were twenty-four school exercises, three unfinished romances, a complete tragedy, written at thirteen years of age, and about forty letters, in a few months, to her mother alone." This statement does not comprise the large proportion (at least one third of the whole) which she destroyed.

The genius of Lucretia Davidson has had the meed of far more authoritative praise than ours. The following tribute is from the " London Quarterly Review," a source whence praise of American productions is as rare as springs in the desert. The notice is by Mr. Southey, and is written with the earnest feeling that characterizes that author, as generous as he is discriminating. " In these poems," (" Amir Khan," etc.) " there is enough of originality, enough of aspiration, enough of conscious energy, enough of growing power, to warrant any expectations, however sanguine, which the patrons, and the friends, and parents of the deceased could have formed."

But, prodigious as the genius of this young creature was, still marvelous after all the abatements that may be made for precociousness and morbid development, there is something yet more captivating·in her moral loveliness. Her modesty was not the infusion of another mind, not the result of cultivation, not the effect of good taste ; nor was it a veil cautiously assumed and gracefully worn ; but an innate quality, that made her shrink from incense, even though the censer were sanctified by love. Her mind was like the exquisite mirror, that cannot be stained by human breath.

Few may have been gifted with her genius, but all can imitate her virtues. There is a universality in the holy sense of duty that regulated her life. Few young ladies will be called on to renounce the Muses for domestic duties; but many may imitate Lucretia Davidson's meek self-sacrifice, by relinquishing some favorite pursuit, some darling object, for the sake of an humble and unpraised duty; and, if few can attain her excellence, all may imitate her in gentleness, humility, industry, and fidelity to her domestic affections. We may apply to her the beautiful lines in which she describes one of those

> —— "forms, that, wove in Fancy's loom,
> Float in light visions round the poet's head."

> "She was a being formed to love and bless,
> With lavish Nature's richest loveliness;
> Such I have often seen in Fancy's eye,
> Beings too bright for dull mortality.
> I've seen them in the visions of the night,
> I've faintly seen them when enough of light
> And dim distinctness gave them to my gaze,
> As forms of other worlds or brighter days."

This memoir may be fitly concluded by the following "Tribute to the Memory of my Sister," by Margaret Davidson, who was but two years old at the time of Lucretia's death, and whom she often mentions with peculiar fondness. The lines were written at the age of *eleven*. May we be allowed to say, that the mantle of the elder sister has fallen on the younger, and that she seems to be a second impersonation of her spirit?

> "Though thy freshness and beauty are laid in the tomb,
> Like the floweret which drops in its verdure and bloom;

Though the halls of thy childhood now mourn thee in vain,
And thy strains shall ne'er waken their echoes again, —
Still o'er the fond memory they silently glide,
Still, still thou art ours, and America's pride.
Sing on, thou pure seraph, with harmony crowned,
  And pour the full tide of thy music along ;
O'er the broad arch of heaven the sweet note shall resound,
  And a bright choir of angels shall echo the song.
The pure elevation which beamed from thine eye,
As it turned to its home in yon fair azure sky,
Told of something unearthly ; it shone with the light
Of pure inspiration and holy delight.
Round the rose that is withered a fragrance remains ;
O'er beauty in ruins the mind proudly reigns.
Thy lyre has resounded o'er ocean's broad wave,
And the tear of deep anguish been shed o'er thy grave ;
But thy spirit has mounted to mansions on high,
To the throne of its God, where it never can die."

NOTES TO AMIR KHAN.

[1] *Beneath calm Cashmere's lovely vale*, &c. "*Cashmere*, called the happy valley, the garden in perpetual spring, and the Paradise of India."

[2] *The bulbul, with his lay of love*, &c. "The Bulbul, or Nightingale."

[3] *The gulnare blush'd a deeper hue*, &c. "Gulnare, or Rose."

[4] *The lofty plane-tree's haughty brow*, &c. "*The Plane-tree*, that species termed *Platanus orientalis*, is commonly cultivated in Cashmere, where it is said to arrive at a greater perfection than in any other country. This tree, which in most parts of Asia is called the *Chinar*, grows to the size of an oak, and has a taper, straight trunk, with a silver-colored bark, and its leaf, not unlike an expanded hand, is of a pale green. When in full foliage it has a grand and beautiful appearance, and in hot weather affords a refreshing shade." — *Foster*.

[5] *And wide the plantain's arms were spread*, &c. "Plantain-trees are supposed to prevent the plague from visiting places where they are found in abundance." — *Middleton's Geography*.

[6] *Knelt the once haughty Subahdar*, &c. "Subahdar, or Governor."

[7] *Since Amir Khan first blessed the hour*, &c. "To the east of this delightful spot is a fortified palace, erected by *Amir Khan*, a Persian, who was once Governor of Cashmere. He used to pass much of his time in this residence, which was curiously adapted to every species of Asiatic luxury." See *Encyclopædia*, vol. v. part 2.

[8] *Through the long walks of tzinnar-trees*, &c.. "Their walks are curiously laid out, and set on both sides with *tzinnar-trees*, a species of poplar unknown in Europe. It grows to the height of a pine, and bears a fruit resembling the chestnut, and it has broad leaves like those of the vine." — *Middleton's Geography*.

[9] *As it glides o'er the wave of the Wuller's stream*, &c. "A beautiful river passes through Cashmere, called the *Ouller*, or *Wuller*. There is an outlet,

where it runs with greater rapidity and force than elsewhere, between two steep mountains, whence proceeding, after a long course, it joins with the Chelum."

[10] *And like a star on Mahmoud's wave*, &c.   "It appears like a lake covered with rocks and mountains. Stones, when thrown in, make a surprising noise, and the river itself is deemed unfathomable." — *Middleton's Geography.*

[11] *Proud Hirney Purvit rears his head*, &c.   "There is an oval lake, which joins the Chelum towards the east. The *Yucht Suliman* and *Hirney Purvit* form the two sides of what may be called a grand portal to the lake. They are hills ; one of which is sacred to the great Solyman."